Love Chemistry

Love Chemistry

And those little reactions!

Shubham Arora

MAHAVEER PUBLISHERS

Published by
MAHAVEER PUBLISHERS
4764/2A, 23-Ansari Road, Daryaganj
New Delhi – 110002
Ph. : 011 – 66629669–79–89
Fax : 011 – 41563419
e-mail : mahaveerpublishers@gmail.com

First Published: August 2011

Love Chemistry
ISBN (10) : 8183520898
ISBN (13) : 9788183520898

Distributed in India by
VAIBHAV BOOK SERVICE
e-mail : vaibhavbookservice@gmail.com

Distributed in Nepal by
BAJRANGBALI BOOK ENTERPRISES PVT. LTD.
Jyatha Mushyabahal, Ward No. 27, Kathmandu, Nepal
e-mail : bajrangbalibooks@gmail.com

Printed by Jaico Printers, New Delhi

Dedication

Papa, Mummy and Aachi,
you are the reason behind my existence.

Acknowledgement

Well, this is it! The time for those thousands of words secretly saved in Microsoft Word to finally arrive on paper, all neat and crisp. Ah, that sounds sweet. This is the page that I always wanted to write once I was at the inception of this book. The motivational factor sort of a thing! And now the moment is there, I would love to put a generous point across anyone and every one who helped and supported me all this while.

First and foremost, this goes to my parents and my dearest sister Mahak (aachi) who have always been firm believers in my abilities and decisions. Without their support, this won't have seen the light of the day.

The second list contains people who I have promised decent enough footage here:

Deepti: Words will always be less when it comes to thanking you. Being the support when I was low! The creativity and enthusiasm you showed while brainstorming over the cover pages has indeed made me a bigger fan of yours.

Rahul: The best of friends and my biggest critic. I don't know if I would have been able to complete my (our) book without your consistent support. Big thanks!

Umang: Ah! I was blessed to have a roommate like you. Truly brother like! The way we used to make our dream castles once I was going to get this published just kept me going.

Aniket, Ankit, Manu, Rachel, Radhika, Atik, Animesh: I would be indebted my entire life for the love and support that you all provided me, not to forget the faith that you always showed. Yeah, using some of the names for the characters definitely helped. I would also like to thank bestselling author Sumrit Shahi who kept me giving insights about publishing.

Ryan International School and Jaipuria Vidyalaya, for being the schools that gave me moments worth cherishing for a life time!

I would love to express my gratitude to the team at Mahaveer Publishers and Mr. Binay for granting me this opportunity and being patient with me throughout the process.

People on my FB friend list and those who feel their names being missed out believe me it's just a matter of space constraints. You can always have me with your complaints and I will in turn make you buy a copy (simple, isn't it?). I have had an amazing experience writing this book. I hope the reading gives you the same!

Preface

I knew no pain
Until I saw yours.
I knew no boundaries
Until I crossed one.
I wasn't an adult
Until I became one!

The vulnerabilities and irrationalities of a young adolescent mind just make this phase of apparent innocence so amazing! Far away from all the hassles in the world, there is a different life that a teenager on the verge of adulthood lives. Though this phase passes and life treads the usual path, the memories of the past stay forever with love and loads of chemistry...

Shubham Arora

Prologue

294

I read it *once again*. It was still 294 printed in Times New Roman against my name. Physics and mathematics were close to average, while chemistry, as always, had been phenomenal. This time I had managed with a negative 0.5 score. I use the word 'phenomenal' because the last time it was a negative 10. I was more careful this time as I attempted only one question in chemistry (that too went wrong) and thus scored a positive 9.5 in comparison to the last time. The truth stared right into my eyes. I was ranked 294th out of 353 students, who had appeared for the exam and it wasn't clearly just about chemistry. It was just that a year had been left and the warning signals were that I had better forget an IIT, or even a decent engineering college if my rendezvous with the exams was going to continue like that.

"I cannot do it, Ma," I announced as soon as I reached home that Sunday morning. It was the same story being repeated every fourth Sunday morning of the month.

"Don't lose heart. You still have another year left. I am sure you will improve," replied Mom as usual in the roundabout manner of saying the same thing at such times. I think it is tough for any mother to accept that her son is no good.

"It has been a year already and you know well what I have been up to," I said, sitting back on the couch in the living room as she brought me a glass of water to drink. "Miracles are confined to mythology books only, Ma. I am not sure about anything."

Mom sat down beside me, gently curling my hair with her hand as I sipped on to the water.

"But you had been performing so well at school. It's just that you have fallen behind in the coaching class. Concentrate a little more; *thoda sa bas.*"

"I can't. You know with the school on and time spent on travelling, it's hard to concentrate in these coaching classes… what can I do here with so many things to do? You have noticed my marks; they haven't got any better."

"Physics and mathematics don't seem that bad. It's just chemistry that worries you, I guess. But see…you have at least improved this time around. It's only negative 0.5."

"That was because I did not attempt anything."

"Okay…so what do we do now? Shall I talk to your Dad about this? If it's bothering you a lot, you can tell us frankly what you want to do. There is no point in carrying it too far."

"I don't want to give up and please don't mention this thing to Dad, otherwise he will get worried," I said, getting up from the couch and moving towards my bedroom. "There is no way out of this. I have to tweak things."

"I guess changing your school might help."

"Can it?" I questioned, halting in my tracks.

"Yes…it should. Something closer to home may help in at least saving your time," Mom said with a confident look on her face.

"I don't know, Mom," I said, sitting back on the couch. "I don't know if that is going to be easy…we can't even be sure if any school will give me admission to Class XII."

"I have got a few contacts, but you must first decide if that is what you want. We can sort the other things as they come up."

I pondered for a couple of minutes, studied the pros and cons and the worst that could happen. It wasn't such a bad deal actually. Saving a couple of hours a day could be a luxury as I could use it for anything.

"Okay…alright…if it can work out that way, I am ready for it."

It had been a year since I had joined that coaching class after giving the entrance exam – an exam to prove if I was worthy of getting admission in such a prestigious organisation that claimed to convert morons into geniuses. A year down and I realised that there was only a hair-line difference between a genius and a moron. Geniuses were those students who could be seen running the classes and morons were the ones like me. The day I got 90 per cent in the Board exam, apart from accepting the congratulations showered on me, the other thing I did was to reply to the question, "What next?"

I clearly remember my chest size increasing an inch every time I would reply proudly, "I want to be an engineer." The reason for saying so, I myself did not know. Maybe every other intelligent ass wanted to be one…maybe after such a percentage, it was expected of me to take up science and mathematics as my core subjects for higher studies…maybe my sister was an engineer, my first cousin, my uncle's daughter, my second cousin, my Dad's uncle's son's son, my seventh cousin, my neighbour, my tenant, everyone was either an engineer or on the path to become one.

"You aren't an engineer unless you do it from an IIT," they all said. Okay, what should I do for it? Give an exam, or loot my father's hard-earned money, or imprison myself in a coaching centre for two years, or lock myself up in a room, or sacrifice my life's little joys because those I could have later…to be into an IIT. And if you aren't, then blame it on either the coaching pattern or the education system.

There was one truth though – I wasn't pushed into the rat race by my parents. I was free to choose what I wanted. I just did not want to look foolish and thus, jumped into the world that I had never seen before. Wait…have you already started thinking about what this story is going to be all about? A loser turning into a hero in the end, doing wonders and performing miracles! That type? *Naah*…this is what it isn't exactly about. Did I not tell my Mom that miracles happen in mythologies only? Right! This hasn't got anything to do with me, a nerd, and turning the world upside down. There will not be any studying strategies or complaints against the education system or fighting my way up the ladder. This is about the little joys of life that I managed to extract on my way through. I switched schools and gave up the last year of my innocence to enter a completely new world, where the days changed my life forever! Welcome aboard to some of the beautiful pages of my life….

P.S.: But after subtracting the studies!

1
The Beginnings are Beautiful

The building with a pink and blue colour combination seemed to be in great shape. The area occupied wasn't large but the surroundings were neat and clean. It was a building with four floors and a large bell, as seen in churches, hung on to a frame on top of the building and was easily visible from the ground. The playground was a little small by normal standards but I consoled my heart by saying that I wouldn't be stepping on to it that often. From the looks of it from outside, I wasn't exactly disappointed. Ryan International School – the large board on the entrance read. The first thing that I discovered in the prospectus before taking admission was that there were another 90 schools in India that associated themselves with this name and a few from abroad were in some collaboration with one another. The second thing that I learnt was that contradictory to the general perception, the school's name wasn't pronounced as 'Reyaan'; it was pronounced as 'Rayan'. It was like saying 'Bryan' without its 'B'. I had got it simpler still…my take was to add an 'an' to a 'Bra' and then remove the 'B'. Not that I was bothered about all this; for me all that mattered was that the school was just a five-minute drive from home and willing to give me some relaxation regarding my attendance. In brief, I found what I wanted.

If I were to say I did not suffer from some uneasiness, a feeling of anxiousness inside my belly that day, I would be hiding the truth. The day my Mom announced that I had been granted admission in this school, my nervous system started giving me the highs. Initially I was apprehensive, but later my apprehensions were replaced by excitement before coming back to apprehension. My feelings were oscillating like a pendulum without coming to rest. There were moments when I felt nostalgic for the school that I was leaving, but the fact that I had spent eleven long years there made me outgrow that with age. So maybe it wasn't that bad an idea to switch schools. Moreover, it was intended to help me out and could not be considered a sacrifice. Obviously, there were a few emotional moments when I told everyone in my old school that I wouldn't be studying with them any more, but it didn't take long for them to get over it, thereby helping my cause.

I was seventeen-years old. I believe it is considered the fag end of teenage and also as the time when a boy starts transforming into a man. Traces of hair on my otherwise bare chest had begun to grow longer, facial hair had become more prominent and I had become aware that my body had begun to secrete certain fluids which made me capable of fathering a baby. This feeling grew manifold with my interest in eves scaling an all-time high. Definitely it was not a great time to prepare for the toughest exam in the nation! But yeah…I was excited as I hoped to see fresh and beautiful faces.

That morning when I entered through the main entrance, neatly clad in that pink checked shirt and khaki trousers (the uniform), I had no idea that I was entering the modern phase of my life. There were little kids running around with some teachers trying to control them, while the more grown up ones were busy chitchatting to each other. It was apparent that the basketball court had been taken over to convert into the area for morning assembly. I made my way into the campus building, walking slowly due to some unknown fear. I was taken aback at the great hustle-bustle inside, with students and teachers vying with each other to flood out of the building. I stopped one boy, who was running out, making a lot of noise with his shoes.

"Excuse me… Class XII science section?" I asked him.

"Yeah…I am in science section. Any problem?" he asked, breathing hard.

"Actually I want to know where the Class XII science section is?" I clarified my point.

"Why? What has happened? I am not telling anyone if there is an extra class today. Tell them yourself."

"I have taken admission this year."

"This year? Bloody dog….are you nuts?" he said, looking straight into my eyes for the first time.

"Ummm…yeah," I said, feeling more embarrassed than confused. My answer evidently was to his first question; or maybe it had answered it all.

"Now I have to go all the way back to the classroom and show you the bloody section. Couldn't you have come a bit earlier?" he turned back and I followed meekly behind him. Aniket Sharma, he told me, was his name. Out of the little information that we exchanged on our way, the most significant that stood out was that he was at the same coaching institute as I. I had never seen him there though. Anyway it's hard to keep track of everyone in a large crowd. The other thing that was worth noticing was the way the stack of hair on his head was arranged. He carried a weird hairdo that must have involved a liberal application of hair oil and it immediately led me to think that if the human species was to get extinct one day and if the scientists of the next originating species were to find this guy's skull as a fossil, they would certainly assume that humans had a huge supply of oil in their hair. Quite foolish but, you see, a thought is a thought!

I entered the classroom, following meekly behind him as he wove his way through a bunch of staring eyes. I kept my eyes down, walking past a few astonished expressions before reaching the last bench where I put my bag down. There were hushed whispers of "who is he?" and similar stuff before, much to my relief, Aniket was seen clearing everyone's doubts on his own. I wondered if I looked like an alien from another planet but consoled myself by saying that it was not every day that people got admission to Class XII straightaway. Naveen, Ankit, Vyom, Dushyant, Suresh…I was still recalling the names that were mentioned while we were getting introduced as I moved along with the entire class to the assembly area. The girls' side was still untouched.

The assembly came as a shocking surprise to me. There wasn't anything unusual about the entire thing apart from one part: the carols. Never before in my life had I sung carols and never before in my life had I danced upon them. And here it was, the entire school dancing together in the name of God. That was something unique to me. I knew I looked stupid while dancing but I can vouch that never had I enjoyed dancing this much before. Everyone, from faculties to kindergarten kids to the XII, everyone was swinging to the rhythm. The first hour certainly did not disappoint me. It wasn't long before we were back in the classroom and I found myself the centre of attraction again. The classroom was divided into two sub-sections, it seemed. The first two rows from the entrance belonged entirely to boys while the other two were occupied by girls. Everyone around was giving me the looks as if they had seen a dead man walking in me. Meanwhile the class-teacher entered the class and I heaved a sigh of relief as everyone got back to his or her own business. The boys seemed friendly, though I was still sitting all alone. My eyes were at times moving towards the other two rows (the girls' side) but hadn't yet found anything eye-pleasing.

"Aadvitya Aurore...you are Roll Number 42," Mr. Chaturvedi, our class-teacher, announced, looking in random directions until I raised my hand and confirmed to him that I was there. Almost all of the class turned back to look at this alien amongst them. I did hear a couple of giggles when the name was announced and I am sure the sound surely originated from the girls' side.

Aadvitya Aurore – I was actually proud of this name that had been given with love by my parents. Though there were a fucking number of objectionable Hindi words that rhymed with my second name, but it always seemed so beautiful to me with my name placed along with it. There are a few celebrities that share the same second name with me and I never miss an opportunity to tell people that there are a few more people who fortunately came in the same category as I. Another unique thing is that it is a palindrome. No matter which way you spell it, forward or backward, it becomes the same again. It hurt actually when someone mispronounced it and this was what I was trying to put across Aniket's brains, when I saw someone at the classroom door. Mr. Chaturvedi was busy introducing the concept of hybridisation in chemistry.

She was late, by a huge margin, considering that even the assembly had got over a long time back. But wasn't she beautiful! She was panting heavily as I saw her seek permission to enter the class. My eyes followed her to the bench where she went and sat down – it was the window side, first bench. Pure beauty! She was moderately tall with long black hair. There was a particular serenity surrounding her fair face which was remarkably spotless. I couldn't have called her sexy but she definitely was cuter than any other thing I had ever seen. A cute metal! There seemed to be nothing existing apart from her in that classroom. My eyes had adopted a periodic movement of their own accord – sometimes they looked at the blackboard, trying to understand the bonding of the 'p' and 's' orbitals, while every other time they gazed at her from their corners. There was a certain aura around her that seemed to brighten everything around her or maybe it was I who was seeing it all from a different frame of mind or it could be the heart! Love at first sight? *Naah*...was that a movie going on? With the advent of testosterone in my blood (or wherever it is), these things were happening within me for every third girl I saw...I immediately shrugged the thought out of my mind, took my eyes off her and started building the molecular orbits along with Mr. Chaturvedi. But man, wasn't she beautiful!

There are people who come into our lives and move away. There are people who come into our lives, stay awhile and we are never the same...

2

Connecting Hearts and Some Souls

The next month or so passed with me in almost complete hibernation. The coaching schedule wasn't allowing me to think about anything else. It was less often that I attended school and thus I was still to develop a strong feeling of belonging to the institute. I had leapt a hundred ranks straight away at the coaching and therefore, my attendance at the school got limited to a mere formality. Life had started getting better already. I had time for myself, the books and every other thing in the world. It wasn't as if I was ignoring school altogether. There were some serious relationships budding, before blossoming enough to spread their fragrance later.

"Aadvitya Aurore…yes, you Aurore?" asked Mr. Chaturvedi, our chemistry and class-teacher with whom I had developed a love-hate relationship. I hated chemistry and as such, I could not have loved him; perfectly justified, this love-hate saga. He too didn't nurture any sympathy for me despite knowing that I was below average at chemistry and thus had fallen victim to daily ordeals or better to say, ordeals which I faced whenever I came to school. This time also he called out my name in the beginning of the lecture and as expected, pronounced it in the most beautiful way that he only could.

"Shit!" I murmured as I stood up from my bench.

"Yeah…so can you tell me...how can we prepare aniline from nitrobenzene?"

"Sir…ummm…no idea," I murmured. Considering my earlier experiences with chemistry, I should have said 'no idea' straight away, but the initial pauses were just a stunt to create an illusion that I might know the answer. It's always great to keep the climax till the end.

"Aurore…I am telling you, you are doing yourself no good. Don't mess around without any use. This guy never comes to school and then replies to nothing. Simply disgusting!" he spat the words as if poisoned or bitter like bitter gourd. He was replying half to me and the other half to the class. There was something that he mumbled under his breath every time he picked on anybody and which I always assumed to be something analogous to an asshole, but nobody had ever heard what he mumbled. Thus my assumptions always remained…well…confined to the zone of assumptions.

"Screw him," I whispered to Aniket as I sat down.

"No…shoot him. I watched the re-run of '*Rang de Basanti*' yesterday again. We should shoot…down…bad…people," Aniket replied, rolling his eyes and dancing his neck.

"Aurore?" I heard the howling voice of Mr. Chaturvedi as I was interrupted in my laughter.

An eternal silence prevailed from my side for the remaining lecture.

Later that day, during recess, a plan was chalked out to go to Nahargarh fort in the evening. I was initially reluctant to go as there was a lot of coaching work still pending but a little bit of emotional blackmailing by Rahul and Manu trapped me in joining them as I decided not to be a spoilsport. I nodded my affirmation by smiling. Rahul Sharma – this guy wasn't in the same section as ours as he had taken biology as an elective, but I got to know him through Aniket. They had been great buddies since the time they both had joined school. It did not take me long to discover that he was almost exactly like me. We relished the same kind of things, got irritated at the same stuff, loved to play the same type of pranks and yeah…loved the same kind of music, and it is said that two men with the same music get along like a house on fire. The same was the case with Manu Pandey, whose senses always were in some different world. There weren't many occasions when I found him being serious about anything. There were probably two things he loved most – shopping without reason and cracking pathetic jokes. His Dad had a business of pharmaceuticals and as Rahul always said, he did not have to carry the cross of building a career on his shoulders. He was born in a silver cradle with a silver spoon in his mouth.

Anyhow, it was fun standing at the classroom door during the recess with them. Simply the best time of the day!

Nahargarh was an ancient fort built high up on the low Aravali hills, traces of which continued on the outskirts of Jaipur. It required a good forty-five-minute journey by road from my house to reach the fort. I did not have any specific information about the place, especially regarding its history apart from the fact that it was built some centuries ago, by the then king of Jaipur to protect the city. One could get a breathtaking view of the Pink City from the top and admire its picturesque beauty. Considering the fact that our all-so-special '*Rang de Basanti*' was shot here with all-so-famous Aamir Khan's sequence of him and Sharman Joshi boozing and falling down from the top, had made this place a serious and rocking hit among the youth here. It was quite famous before also, but somehow the frequency of visits by people like us had increased considerably over the past few months.

So that evening, I took Aniket along with me after the coaching classes got over. Rahul and Manu were to reach directly and meet us up at the fort only. It took us a while to escape the city traffic before reaching the mountainous path that led to the fort. It was around 8 in the night.

I had never been to the fort that late in the night. All along the journey, we didn't come across a single road light along the path. "Bloody politicians, eating away my Dad's money; haven't bothered to put a single road light along the way. What is the chance that we will not fall down the valley?" Aniket blabbered, while seated behind me on my bike. I did not pay much heed to what he said as my attention was more towards the road that lay ahead and on balancing the bike on the uphill slope where I couldn't run beyond the third gear. I knew that the fort was open only till 5 in the evening. Maybe that's why no road lights had been installed on the path. It, however, could not be denied that people enjoyed visiting the place only at night and therefore, there was always some news of someone or other falling off the hill.

In a little while, we reached our destination. As expected, the fort was closed but we weren't much concerned about it. There were a few open places where one could sit and look around at the beautiful images of the city below. The place was dead dark, except for the little lights that were blinking in the city below. I parked my bike at a vacant spot and started searching for Manu and Rahul. We both were yet tying to adjust our vision to the darkness around when I chose to switch off the ignition key as also the headlights.

"If we have been brought here on a fool's errand, I swear I will surely screw them up tomorrow," Aniket threatened, his emotions coming to the fore.

"Wait...let me call them up and check," I replied, taking my cell phone out of my pocket.

"Shit...no network! Let's move to that *baoli*...Rahul had told me to wait over there," I said, moving towards it as Aniket followed behind me. He was chanting something continuously in his mouth but I didn't bother to listen. As I moved down the steps to the *baoli*, I still couldn't see anything clearly except for the reflection of the moon in the water stagnating below on the ground. In the daylight this place looked awesome but I realised that the mysterious night light added to its beauty here and there. With my little historic knowledge about the place, I could recall that this was the place where royal queens and princesses used to take a bath when they were alive. The mere thought of gorgeous young ladies bathing in the *baoli*, filled me with an unusual sense of excitement. I fantasied that some day I might end up seeing the royal ghosts (and that too some pretty ones) taking a dip in the water. Human race never stops imagining, you see!

"Whoooooha...!" Rahul screamed from behind, waking me up from my fantasy sleep.

"Doggy…we were searching for you like anything!! And Pandey…keep your dirty yellow 28 teeth inside your stinky mouth. We did not even feel like screaming out of fear!" Aniket said, catching hold of Manu's neck. Rahul stood leaning against the wall built around the *baoli*. He was hiding something behind him but I did not pay much attention to it.

"How long has it been since you both reached here?" I queried, sitting upon the platform built around the stagnant water.

"Rahul forced me to come over here early. We came here around 6:45 p.m. I guess. This guy is such an asshole I tell you," said Manu for the first time. I noticed it was him now who was holding Aniket's neck. I couldn't stop myself from smiling over the game that was going on between the two of them.

"We had to come early to make all the arrangements, you see," Rahul said, sitting beside me now and I could clearly see what he was hiding behind his back. It was a chiller, a big one which could possibly hold around fifteen to twenty bottles at a time.

"Alcohol?" I asked with amazement.

"Fool…not every bottle holds booze! These are just soft drinks," Rahul replied. Manu and Aniket had joined us after playing enough of their acts.

"Cheers then!" I said, taking one of the bottles and holding it up in the air, as others followed to do the same.

"Guys...seriously, I have been to this place quite a few times before, but I must admit it never looked so pretty before. I have never come here at night, but tonight, as I sit here talking to you people, I feel I am having the best time of my life. It's all so soothing and calm out here. It's so...it's so...I mean I just can't find a word to describe this place." I must have sounded completely awestruck when I said these words.

"It's so…it's so....romantic *naah*. I told you Rahul, this guy isn't straight. I told you before also and I have known it from the very beginning...!" replied Manu, imitating me.

"Ha! Ha! Ha!...I appreciate your genius, Manu," Rahul added.

"Shut up," I said for I knew my leg was being pulled and I was trying my best to get out of it. I just smiled back at them and began to look up in the sky, trying to avoid their eyes.

"Speak Arori...speak *naah*, Doggy!" said Aniket, definitely not in the mood to spare me from this. He had developed his own way of calling me by my second name. I did not look towards him and continued to gaze up in the sky.

Chhamma chhamma...baaje re meri paijaniya...

Chhamma chhamma...

That seemed like the ring tone of a cell phone. Yes, it was Aniket's cell phone, I noticed. It was pretty obvious that his cell had caught the network.

"Fucking shit, dude! When are you going to change this ear-crushing thing? Yuck!" Rahul yelled and I found it quite funny the way he screwed his nose and face while saying the words.

"What? It's so cool...*yah*...hello...*jaanu*..." replied Aniket, picking up the phone and ambling away from us before fading into the dark. Aniket, I was told, had a girlfriend since the time he was a kid. When I was busy trying to fathom the difference between a guy and a girl in my tender years, he was busy formulating the love quotient somewhere. It was since Class VIII that he had been going around and it had been more than a year since his girl had left school. Obviously with the introduction of the female phenomenon, I knew questions would be raised.

"Do you like someone?" Rahul asked me (Bingo, I was right!). He loved to probe his nose into other people's affairs. The biggest myth to be associated with *Homo sapiens* is that guys don't gossip!

"Not yet!" I replied.

"Sure?" Rahul asked, raising an eyebrow.

"Absolutely…I have no reason to hide anything from you people," I said, trying my best to reassure them. "Haven't felt that way for any girl so far," I was quick to add.

"Okay…you don't like anyone here? I mean our school.... your new school..." Manu butted in, preparing for the second round of the leg-pulling session.

"Nope…not really," I replied, sounding absolutely disinterested while sipping my soft drink. It was my third of the evening already.

"Not really? I see. I tell you…there are two things that I will love to share with you," Manu said, sipping a few drops himself as he spoke.

"Yeah, speak it out," I replied.

"First thing…I like that Carol from the commerce section and Rahul likes her best friend, Mallya…so if you like either of them, forget both of them."

"Second thing…I know there is someone from your class... I have noticed you, dude a few times. It's just that I haven't been able to figure out. Now that I have shared mine and Rahul's secret with you, it will be better for you to come out clean," Manu said, winking towards Rahul, who was doing nothing except to smile.

"It's nothing like that. I like her…yeah…I can say this much, I find her cute enough..."

"Speak out the name *yaar,*" Rahul said, interrupting me in between.

"I...I don't know the name yet and believe me, it's nothing like what you people think," I said hesitantly, trying to put my point across vehemently.

"You don't know the name? Strange! Rahul...it's that nymphomaniac fatso again. Like others, it seems he has fallen for her too, I am sure," Manu said, passing his verdict with full confidence.

"Fuck off! She isn't a fatso…she is so damn beautiful," the very mention of the words like 'fatso' and 'nymphomaniac' were enough to upset me.

"That's it, you ass...we got it. You bloody well like her!" Rahul said excitedly, patting my back.

I realised what a stupid mistake I had made by replying to Manu. 'What the fuck?' I said to myself.

"So who is she?" Manu asked like a pain in the neck.

"I don't know...she sits on the second bench near the window. I just find her beautiful…that's it, believe me," I said, desperately trying to convince them that there was nothing more to it.

"Ohhhh…Noopur? Nice girl...interesting choice," Rahul said teasingly.

"I just find her beautiful, that's it! Nothing else *yaar*," I said, hoping to convince them.

"Yeah…we know…c'mon, let's go back now…it's already 10:30. We will be definitely reprimanded at home if we return later than this," said Rahul, standing up from the platform as we noticed Aniket reappear on the scene.

"But I did not say that I liked her," I continued to explain my position.

"C'mon now, we will think about that later," Manu said, catching my hand and pulling me up from the platform.

"What has happened?" Aniket queried.

"Nothing…I'll tell you on our way back home. Let's go now," I replied before anyone could start offering his own version.

Aniket and I picked up our bags and all of us started to move towards our bikes, with all the three excitedly discussing something among themselves as I walked slowly behind, lost in my own thoughts. Though I could make out that one name was being oft repeated – 'Noopur.'

3

My First Kiss…

"Yeah…yeah, Parv…yeah...do one 500 for me," said Aniket into the receiver. "Yeah right…I will come to see you at night. Okay, 'bye," he said and put down the phone.

"I heard 500…what was that?" I asked out of curiosity.

"Nothing…just a mobile recharge. I asked Parv to do it for me," he replied.

"Seems like it's going to be a long talk with Neha today… huh?" I said, trying to tease him.

"I can always talk for long as it doesn't cost too much. For today, it's all free!" he replied smilingly.

"Free? How? Parv has opened some mobile shop or what? Is this a treat for you? Where is mine, then?" I asked.

"No…it's nothing like that. He knows a few hacking tricks actually, so he makes these for free. I have asked him a few times to let me know how it is done, but the doggy that he is, I tell you, he will never ever reveal his secret. He says he gets it done through a friend of his but doesn't know a thing about it himself.

Such a genius he is, man!" Aniket replied to my question. I knew he went a little overboard with that genius title for Parv but knowing Aniket, it was common for him to make ordinary people seem eminent.

"Ohhh…is that true? Then I will ask him to make one for me some day; nothing better than a few hundred bucks of free balance," I said, trying to sound overjoyed.

I was amazed though how Aniket was in close contact with this guy. He was the most ugly duckling I had ever seen in my life; I mean, he was nothing but ugly. He had a lanky physique with a dark body that could put the blackest of shoes to shame. The squint in his eyes was covered with a sparkling red pair of spectacles that added to his unconventional beauty remarkably. I know calling someone 'black' is close to being racist but seriously, it was because of his deportment that he seemed uglier than anything else. It wasn't as if I was in the habit of judging people by their physical appearance. I had seen uglier people than him, but somehow when I looked at him, I was reminded of filth. This guy's very presence around me used to piss me off like anything. All those initial days at the school, I had noticed, he had been busy trying to get close to all of us despite realising that nobody really bothered about him. He had joined the school only a year earlier than me but had no good friends so far. He never had an interesting piece of story to tell and neither did he possess any great sense of humour to draw the attention of others. He was like the so-called *chipko* that nobody wanted around. I wondered why he never understood that we did not want him. Now, the realisation that Aniket was actually on talking terms with him, made me greet him with a gaping mouth. But that whole free recharge phenomenon had made me understand everything.

"He is such a nice and helpful guy," Aniket began.

"That he is," I replied forcefully.

Beep…beep…beep!

Aniket's cell phone had been recharged. For my satisfaction, I threw a glance at his mobile screen and it flashed that it had been recharged with 500 rupees worth of balance.

"Now please don't start talking right now. Drop me home first…" I said to him. We had started going to the coaching class together and were on our way back home when we stopped on the way for Aniket to talk to Neha (his girlfriend). I had been a victim of this quite a lot of times already when he used to stand on the road for hours, talking to his lady love and I would sit on his scooter, waiting for him. The scene never changed even if we took my bike to the institute. The only difference was that my bottoms felt better, comforting themselves on my bike seat. It wasn't that bad a deal initially as it helped me to indulge in bird watching but after some time, I realised that it was actually a waste of a lot of time. It was much better to head back home and take a nap (yeah...at times I tried being a nerd).

I slept a good two hours after reaching home. I would have woken up early next morning, only if Mom hadn't woken me up to announce that my friends were waiting downstairs. I stood up from my bed with half-open eyes and noticed from the balcony that Aniket and Parv stood waiting for me.

"Mom…you could have sent them back," I said in a distressed voice. Mom just gave me a helpless look in return.

"Okay…I'll be back soon. Let the food be ready till then," I said and rushed downstairs.

"Hey Arori!" Parv screeched, his voice on full throttle as soon as he saw me.

"Hey!" I replied. *Asshole!* I knew the next few minutes were going to be the most boring ones. I could have made a thousand different expressions at that time and all of them would have expressed the same one thing – DISGUST.

"You don't seem to be in a great mood," Parv commented.

You are depriving someone of his beautiful dreams and yet you expect him to be in a great mood, huh!

"*Naah*...I am fine," I replied.

"Come on Arori. Let's go and drink some milkshake," Aniket suggested, starting his scooter.

"I don't feel like having anything right now. Maybe some time later." *Or never.* I seriously did not want to go and waste my precious time on drinking some boring milkshake.

"We came specially to meet you, *sahib*...and you are not at all in a positive state of mind. What is this Aniket? Arori *sahib*, you are such a big bore?" Parv *sahib* said, adjusting his spectacles and twisting his neck sideways.

His each word was making me feel more irritated than ever and this outburst of friendliness and authority over me left me more rankled than ever before. There wasn't any special reason to hate him but he was just like those 'straight out of animal planet' kind of creature whom you just could not help but hate. His thoughts were unimpressive and uninspired. My heart was overflowing with 'fuck his mother and sister' abuses.

"What Arori? Parv has come only for your sake. Don't be an asshole now. *Chal*," Aniket said. He couldn't have been more sympathetic. *And asshole? Me? What about that black hole that was right there gawping towards me? Fucker.*

"Okay...let's go, but not for too long. I have to study," I said and went and sat on Aniket's scooter, grateful to my books for helping me serve as an excuse.

"Arora *sahib*...my pillion is also vacant. You can come here too." I don't need to mention who could have said that. I would have killed him right there, only if he used that fucking *sahib* one more time.

'Shut up you *sisterfuck,'* my lips were about to form as my heart had been churning within me for long.

Exactly five minutes later we reached the parlour. Actually the word 'parlour' would be an overstatement. It was a local juice shop on the roadside which offered milkshakes along with fruit juices and here I was, going to sip the most boring shake of my life with this lunatic.

"I heard you are into hacking and all?" I began as we sat down.

"Who told you that?" he counter-questioned me. I pointed towards Aniket, who was rolling his eyes from left to right and vice versa, watching every girl pass on the crossroads. He was ogling, to be precise.

"Ohhh…that? Yeah…a bit of…just these recharges and stuff. Actually one of my friends knows a lot about it, so it helps."

"Okay," I said. There was a silence for two minutes till Aniket said, "Parv…why don't you get Aadi recharged?"

"Ah…*haan*…yeah…I will…right now," he said, hesitating for a moment. I kept quiet as none of my senses urged me to say 'no'. I would not have objected to a free recharge; at least that would have compensated for the time wasted on this black hole.

"Take my number then. It's 99…"

"I know," he replied. I was surprised that this alien knew my number too.

He messaged something from his mobile to someone and within five minutes I received a message that accounted for a debit of rupees hundred from my balance. Just a hundred bucks worth of balance; I wouldn't have minded a 500-bucks lottery, asshole!

"Thanks," I said, trying not to look dejected.

"The shake bill is on you, Arori...something in return," Aniket said.

"Yeah...doesn't matter," I said. The bill amounted to sixty rupees, so it was a profit of forty rupees for me (yeah...Jaipur is cheap if you are willing to feast on roadside *dhabas* for the shakes). It was some profit at least.

"So Aadi, do you remember Chicki?" Parv asked all of a sudden.

"Who?" I was shocked for a starter. I was getting so used to that *sahib* word that it actually took me a while to realise that his question was addressed to me.

"Your childhood friend, with whom you used to spend a lot of time. Now, can you recall?" he asked, twisting his neck like a lunatic again.

I remember perfectly, asshole! Chicki, as told to me by my Mom, was my best childhood friend. He used to live in my neighbouring flat and we used to have a blast of a time together. As we were about to complete our Montessori, his father got transferred and they moved to Ajmer. I am told that I wept for two days, continuously pestering my Mom to get him back, which eventually never happened. When I was in Class III, my family and I went for a trip to Ajmer where I met him again and that was the last I remember of seeing him.

Wait...he can't be Parv...no...no...I remember Chicki having a dark complexion; but was he that dark?

"H...how...how do you know him?" I asked, keeping my fingers crossed. Deep within, I was fervently praying that he should not turn out to be the same Chicki...please.

"Because I am Chicki only...your childhood friend."

Fuck, a heavy truck passed down the road and I had the urge to jump right in front of it and be crushed to pieces. This weirdo was my best friend at one time...shit...shit...shit. I have always had these kinds of complaints with God – events that we consider avoidable in life come to stare at us right in our eyes at some stage or other. I have had complaints against my average-looking face too, but what seemed more ridiculous was to find the freaking ass turn out to be one of my best friends and I did not want that. Damn...why did I have to come out with him? I was better off sleeping.

"Ohhhh…nice to see you here," I said, trying to act normal. I could not have been more expressive than this. I was probably shocked; not *probably*, in fact, I was far greatly shocked.

"I am so happy to see you here. The moment I saw your house, I knew it was you…I knew it was you," he said. *Did I see his eyes get wet under those spooky glasses of his? Emotional fool!*

"Yeah, yeah," I said, wishing to be colder than that.

"Have you guys done with your *bharat milaap*? We need to head back home. My Mom has been screaming over the phone," Aniket said, standing up from his chair. I paid the bill and headed towards Aniket's scooter.

"Oye Arora…I have to head back straight home; my Mom will tear me into pieces otherwise. You go with Parv, who will drop you on his way," Aniket said.

Screw you, man! I looked towards Parv and noticed him sitting on his bike, giving me that ugly smile. I hated that...seriously. I had no other option, but to move towards his bike.

"I am not in a mood to drive. Do you mind driving?" Parv asked.

I took the keys from him and started the bike.

"Where do you live?" I asked him, while driving his bike.

"Swarn Path…at the students' hostel! It's just a hundred metres away from your house," he replied.

"When did you come back to Jaipur?" I asked, simply to break the uncomfortable silence during the ride.

"Last year only! Dad sent me back here to study. It feels so great being back again...being with you...," he said.

I did not ask anything else; in any case I did not want to actually. My home was just a few metres away and I was more than happy at the fact that I would be able to go back to sleep and enjoy seeing all the beautiful dreams I had been seeing before leaving home.

That was until he said, "It's so much fun being with you all."

Pucchhhhhhhhh!!!!

Fuck...fuck...dickhead...black hole! That bloody moron had placed his all-black lips on my cheeks and given me a saliva-loaded kiss. Fucker! I was literally shocked. I applied the brakes and got off. Yuck...he had kissed me. Maybe that was a friendly one but still it was a kiss and that too from him! I punched him with a fist full of strength right on his stomach. He kept on laughing like an idiot. Was he deliberately making it look like a joke?

"Arse...stay away and buzz off from here before I cut you into pieces. Just bloody fuck off....you moron," I screamed at him. He continued to laugh. I pushed him with my hand on his chest to convey that I did not want him there any more. He kick started his bike and zoomed away, laughing loudly. I started walking back home on foot. All the way I had to experience his stinky, shitty, salivary smell hitting my nostrils. It was the first time that I observed that saliva smelled like shit. I felt damn disgusted and kept on hurling abuses at him. My mouth had puked quite often that day...and it continued to do so till I reached home. I rushed towards the washbasin to wipe my cheek clean and started rubbing it furiously.

"What's happened?" asked my Mom.

I had nothing to say. All I said was, "Nothing…just some dirt…"

4

All about Love, Trains and Abuses

I woke up the next morning with my alarm clock letting out a shrill scream. I checked the time; it was 7:30 already. Considering the fact that the school began at 7:45, I was obviously late without doubt. So without wasting any more time, I jumped out of the bed and straightaway headed towards the bathroom.

The previous evening had been quite an experience. My mind began to replay what had happened. I began to wonder if I was being rather suspicious and doubtful and felt somewhat guilty as if I had behaved in an improper manner and mistaken a friendly gesture in an absurd way. Even girls blow kisses at each other (I knew I was too liberal about the usual cheeky girls). So maybe it wasn't a big deal and I might have overreacted. After returning home late, I had got down to completing the leftover work given at my coaching class and went to sleep real late. I am not amongst those who can beat sleep. So the extra hours that were spent the previous night were compensated by getting up late the next morning.

I checked out on my wristwatch as I took out my bike. It was 7:45. I was happy that I had saved a few minutes by not having a bath and only dry-cleaning myself inside the bathroom (more so by the fact that at least I was able to clean up my bowels within a record time).

As I drove towards the school, I noticed it was a beautiful morning. The sky was overcast and it seemed a certainty that it was going to rain. My heart somewhat sank, as I parked my bike in the school, at the thought of being confined within the four walls of the classroom on such a heart-warming morning.

I had missed the first lecture by the time I reached the classroom; the next period was of English language. I always loved English literature and grammar. Not that I was being partial to the language; it was simply because I felt that English was based on human thoughts, it was about interpreting things, it wasn't about logics and better still, it wasn't chemistry. Moreover, I used to get better marks in English compared to other subjects. And as they say, marks are equivalent to respect in the eyes of the teachers; all my life I had found it easier to impress the English lecturers. They were always beautiful and the most intellectual of the lot.

Miss Chandrakanta entered the classroom. I was yet to be included in her exceptional students' list as my attendance in school had so far been as good as negligible. I looked out of the window and noticed raindrops falling on the basketball court outside. I looked all over the ground and noticed people upbeat with excitement as if gearing up to hold a picnic. Studying in such a joyous ambience wasn't any bad either, I thought.

"The girl on the second bench...yeah, you...start reading the third chapter aloud and all the others please concentrate on your books. I can ask anyone to explain what she would have read,"

Miss Chandrakanta announced as I withdrew my eyes from the scene outside to take out the book from my bag.

And then my eyes fell on something amazing. Gosh, she was the same girl that Manu and Rahul had been discussing that night at Nahargarh. I had intentionally stopped looking at her since the past few days, but now she was seated right there on the second bench. My eyes just couldn't blink. From what I could see, she was looking dangerously pretty and then she started reading.

Heavens!! It was raining outside but I was hearing temple bells ring right inside my ears as if playing an orchestra of violins, guitars, pianos – all beautiful sounding stuff seemed like playing just for me. She was reading and I was listening – listening to her baby-like voice: so innocent. The peace that existed inside my mind at that moment could not be measured. I knew it was quite the Bollywood style, but could I deny the fact that it was happening in real to me? That voice was so soothing; I felt that it was having some divine effect on me. I had never heard such a voice like this ever. Was it because of the rain or was it because of her, I was simply getting lost? What was happening?

"Aadi…oye…Aadi!" I heard someone calling my name.

"Ah…Ah…*Haan,*" I spoke as if waking up from a long hibernation.

"Ass…ma'am is calling you." I realised it was Aniket whispering.

"Yes, the guy at the last! Start reading from where she left," and now I could hear the other voices clearly. It was I who was supposed to start reading.

"Sorry ma'am...I can't," I stood up from my bench and replied. Being in my full senses, I could not have made a reply better than this.

"Why do you even come to school?? You won't be attending my next lecture and don't even bother to say a sorry to me… no…no…no sorry at all." Miss Chandrakanta could not proceed with her banging further as the short bell rang for recess and she left, furious.

"*You'll bloody well like her, dude*!" Rahul's words from that night came to strike into my mind.

As everyone prepared to take out their lunch-boxes and go outside in the rain, I looked at her for a second and immediately looked away. The only words to come out of my mouth were, "Sheeh, man!"

* * * * *

"Aadi…I need your help, dude!" said Manu, panting on the phone.

"What's happened?" I asked.

"I am in a mess. I do not know what to do. She is going away. She is actually going away to never come back. Fuck…I cannot do anything about it."

"Hey…calm down and tell me what exactly has happened?" I asked him.

It took him some time to explain to me the entire scenario. Carol, his lady-love from the commerce section was going away to Mumbai. Her Dad had got transferred and therefore, the entire family was shifting to Mumbai. It meant she was going to leave Jaipur as also her school midway in Class XII. Since Ryan International School had around hundred branches across India, changing school was no problem as a transfer certificate would have easily got her admission in its Mumbai branch. But this was not what worried Manu. His problem was related to the fact that she was going far away from him and there was nothing that he could do about it.

"She doesn't even know how much I like her. She cannot even imagine the pain that I am feeling. Why did she tell me this only on the day of her departure?"

"Is she leaving today? Don't tell me that," I replied with amazement.

"Yeah…she is! Today at 2:00 p.m. by the *Jaipur-Mumbai Superfast Express*! It seems she had been in a hurry to leave that prompted her to travel by this superfast train. There are so many trains from which she could have chosen but she had to choose this train. God knows why this should be happening to me?" he said, sobbing loudly over the phone. I knew that his reason for depression was not that the train was 'superfast'; it was that he would not be able to see her again.

"Damn it! Just tell her what you feel about her before she departs. Call her right now and tell her that you like her. Don't waste time talking and weeping like this; just bloody well call her up," I said, from whatever experience I had of such cases. Such cases had been frequently depicted in most of the Bollywood movies, so my advice emerged from my experience of the big screen.

"You think so? I should call her?" he asked, his sobs coming to a halt all of a sudden. He really had taken my advice seriously.

"I think so," I replied convincingly. There was nothing else that I could think of telling him. .

"Yeah…I think I have to do it right now. Yeah…I am going to do it," he said, sounding determined.

"That's the spirit. Go on."

Manu put down the phone and I was relieved to find that I could solve his problem without getting unduly entangled. I had no desire to spoil my three-day long break from both the school and the coaching institute. Since the state elections were scheduled to take place, the entire state had been given a break. This gave me the opportunity to re-analyse where I stood in the competition for entry into the IITs and NITs and work towards improving my standing. Some of the pending assignments had yet to be completed. At times, studying isn't such a bad thing provided you are in the right mood for it. In any case, my moods were in proper shape only on occasions that were few and far between in any academic year. So I felt quite upbeat about the three-day break.

Rahul had gone to his relatives in Delhi and Aniket had been forbidden by his parents to leave home. It was still early days for Parv to be counted amongst us. So it was like heaven for me as this meant fewer chances of interruption to my study programme. I had already begun to imagine securing a higher rank in the forthcoming exams. The first day of holidays passed peacefully but on the second day, I received a call from Manu. Apparently with no Rahul or Aniket around, it left me only for him to contact and share his problem. Anyway, I was glad that I could provide him some solution and did not allow his depression to affect me. I was preparing for another date with my books when the phone rang. It was Manu again.

"Aadi...I need your help," he said breathlessly.

"Now what has happened?" I asked resignedly.

"I did not say anything to her. As I was not sure how she would react to my overture, I did not talk to her on the phone. I have to meet her before she leaves. I have to..."

"But how is that possible? Her parents will be present with her. As she is leaving today, she will be busy packing her stuff," I said.

"Her parents have already gone. She is travelling all alone and has already finished with her packing. Her parents left for

Mumbai a week ago. She has stayed behind to spend some more time with her friends. I have a plan…," he said.

"What plan?" I asked, putting my books aside. I knew, with his long-winded plans, books were the last thing he would touch that day.

"I am meeting her at the railway station. I have made all the arrangements. I want to meet her and say all that I have been treasuring inside my heart for so long."

"Then go, asshole. What are you waiting for?" I said, heaving a sigh of relief that I could go back to my books again.

"You need to come with me. I cannot go all alone. It scares me. I need your support Aadi…you've got to accompany me." His voice was tinged with worry and apprehension and despite longing to turn him down, I had to relent to his demand.

He picked me up at 1:30 from my house. Since I was in no mood to drive my bike, I had asked him to pick me up from home. It did two things: saved me fuel and my energy (*only to spoil it later*). On the way, I discovered that we were not going to the main Jaipur junction but were headed towards the less crowded and nearer to home Durgapura Railway Station (*and no, it isn't a fort in Jaipur*). The Mumbai train halted for only two minutes at this station, the reason for which my brain failed to decipher. The train used to take only ten minutes to reach the station from the main junction. I began to wonder why Manu had chosen to meet her here when he could have gone straight to the main station, where he could have spent more time with her.

We reached the railway station at exactly 2 o'clock. About ten minutes were left for the train to arrive. The station wore a deserted look and then it struck me that this could be the reason for Manu to choose this place for declaring his love to her. I was treated to a Coke to pass my time and I happily sipped on it.

All the while I noticed tha.t Manu kept on putting his hand in and out of the bag that he carried with him. The train arrived on the station, blowing its horn when I noticed a strange sparkle in Manu's eyes. I saw him walk briskly towards her coach. I followed him. She was standing right there on the door.

"Hey!" she said.

"Hey!" Manu replied.

"Hey!" I said but there was no response because who could be interested in greeting me. She was leaning on the door as Manu stood on the platform with me behind him. I noticed she was wearing a pink T-shirt with a pair of rugged blue denims. She was from the commerce group and thus I hadn't noticed her in school. She was dark complexioned and far from those angel-like beauties one sees on and off, but she seemed to make up for her drawback by dressing and carrying herself smartly. At least that is what my first impression conveyed.

"Manu…it's just two minutes," I whispered. He did not care to listen because he was so much into her.

"I did not expect you to come here. I thought you must be joking," she said to Manu.

"I had to come," Manu replied. After a minute, he added, "I hope you had no problem in reaching the station." I had been waiting for him to say these words.

"*Naah*…aunty was with me," she replied.

"So…when will you be back from Mumbai?" he asked, his hand still inside his bag. *Say it, damn it!*

"I don't know. Maybe never! We have no relatives here…. so maybe I will not come back ever," she said with a smile, possibly to hide her real feelings. The next thirty seconds or so went, with both of them just looking away from each other. Is that what was called love? Was she expecting him to say something? I knew Manu had lost it. The very thought of her not coming back had made him dumbfounded. Wasn't he going to say what he had been longing to say? I stood watching them look away from each other when the train honked loudly. The two minutes were over. *Say it, you asshole. What are you waiting for?* The train started moving slowly off the platform but he stood still, like a mute guy. *Say it, moron!*

"Bloody well tell her what is up your ass, idiot!" I screamed.

"What?" she exclaimed, as the distance between her and us began to increase.

I think my words jolted him out of his reverie and he started running, with me behind him as the train began to gather momentum. While both of us were running, suddenly something happened, which was well beyond my imagination!

"Fucker, do you have any idea as to what we have done? We are on a train to Mumbai without any tickets in our hands. You ran and climbed into the train and unmindful of what you were up to, I followed suit and now we are screwed, you ass," I screamed.

"I could not have let you go like this Carol," he was saying to her. *Was I invisible?* He had not heard a single word of what I had said. I pinched myself to check if I was alive and had not become a ghost on catching the train.

"What?" she asked, looking shocked to find us both in her coach. Even I was no less shocked!

"I love you, Carol. I really do. For the past ten years, since I came to my senses, it has been only you that I have admired, adored and cared for. It was my fault for not saying this to you before but now that you are leaving forever, I cannot stop myself from saying that I love you." Aha...thank God...at least he did say that, though I was still worried about travelling without a ticket.

"What?" I noticed she was shocked, but had he not made it plain and clear? He loved her. But then, a girl cannot be a girl without putting on all these pretensions, you see.

"I love you Carol," he repeated, putting his hand inside his bag and pulling out a soft toy on which was written, 'I LOVE YOU' in bold and capital letters. Soon a few chocolates followed from the ubiquitous bag.

We were still standing close to the door with a strong wind blowing across our faces because of the fast speed of the train. I took one look at her face and noticed it turn blank. Manu's face resembled a beggar's, expecting money. It was another case that he was begging for love. She looked away and suddenly a blush accompanied with a smile began to play on her face. Her cheeks went all pink (okay, as I told you before, she was dark but pink was visible on the dark skin). She turned back, taking the soft toy from Manu's hand.

"I never knew you had it in you to say this. Idiot, you could have said this before also…why did it take you so long to say this?" she asked with tears glistening in her eyes. I knew that any moment her tears would begin to flow down. Every emotional scene in the world is depicted through them.

"Could be because I had never expected you to leave me and go away!" Manu said and they both hugged each other. After all, they were conventional people, you see.

I looked away. *Damn it, we were without tickets.*

"I love you too," I heard her say. They both, with their hands locked in each other's, sat down on the steps that led to the door of the coach and started enjoying the outside view. I knew they were in love but the ticket-checker was not and he could appear any moment to put an end to their love story.

"Oye Manu…are we going to Mumbai too?" I asked, interrupting their love overtures.

"Nope dude…the next station is Sanganer. It's just ten minutes from here…we will get down there. Till then, chill…and enjoy the scenery outside." I was glad that he had actually heard me this time. Still holding each other's hands, Carol had rested her head on his shoulder. I wondered what they were talking about but I was comforted by the fact that it was only another ten minutes and we would be off the train. I went and opened the opposite door to the one they were sitting near and sat down on the small steps, supporting my legs on them. I was finally happy that Manu had been able to reveal his true feelings to her and spend some valuable time together.

I sat on the steps for five minutes when the train zoomed past some small station. As the train passed by, out of sheer curiosity, I looked at the board to find the name of the station. I saw Sanganer written on it. I jumped up and began to shout and scream.

"Asshole…did you notice which station it was? Sanganer is gone. The train did not stop and we are screwed...screwed big time. You are having a gala time here while I will get my ass stuffed today. What am I going to tell Mom? That I am accompanying Manu to Mumbai to help him get his lady love…Fuck you, Manu!"

Manu was expressionless. He too had stood up from where they were seated. She still looked shocked but that was probably due to the amount of abuses I had hurled at her boyfriend.

"You sure it was Sanganer?" Manu asked calmly. They were still holding hands.

"I have fucking eyes to see that, moron! I wonder where this train will halt next," I said, fuming with anger. Being calm was the last thing to expect from me at that point of time.

"If it hasn't halted at Sanganer, then the next stop is only Sawai Madhopur, baby…That means we get some more time together…this day is lucky for me," Manu replied, looking towards her.

"More time? How far is Sawai Madhopur from here?" I asked, losing all my cool and peace of mind. His unconcerned look was serving to add fuel to the fire burning inside me.

"It is only two-and-a-half hours from here," he said, sitting down again on the steps with his ladylove and their hands locked in each other's. If only I had a knife with me, I would not have taken a single moment to think but pierced his heart there and then. I would have chopped him into pieces and thrown the dead body on the railway track on which my train was moving. I was inflamed. I wanted to scream, cry, screech and shriek, though I was aware that it would have no effect. Manu was totally lost. Two-and-a-half hours meant a hell of a lot of time and I realised that I had not much strength left to crib any further. I lapsed into deadly silence; in any case, what alternative did I have? For once, I thought of jumping off the train but taking into account the short life that I had spent so far and not yet accomplished any of my goals, I decided not to take the risk.

I went and took Carol's ticket from her and rang up Mom, making the excuse that I was getting some notes xeroxed and would therefore get late in reaching home. I then entered the compartment for the first time since so far I had been standing or sitting near the doorway. Fear of the ticket collector's arrival soon vanished from my mind as I resigned myself to my fate. I looked around, but found not a single hot female species anywhere in the hundred square feet area around me. So taking a short two-hour nap wasn't such a bad idea. In any case I could not have done anything except that. I lay down comfortably on the upper berth and surrendered myself to sleep.

"Aadi…wake up…it's time to get down. Climb down…fast," I heard him say as I opened my eyes. I glanced at my wrist-watch and found it was fifteen minutes past five. It took me a few seconds to realise that it was Manu who had spoken those words.

"How come that no ticket collector came?" I asked him as I jumped down from my berth.

"I will tell you later. Right now…let's go," he replied.

I turned back to look behind me and noticed her still standing in the doorway, smiling at Manu. She was looking beautiful but that smile had cost me so much of my energy and time that I was in no mood to appreciate it. I was the first one to get down from the train. I did not look back as I noticed Manu taking his own sweet time to follow me. I could guess that possibly they had kissed each other before parting company. In any case, I was least concerned or interested in them. I wanted to get back home as fast as I could and nothing mattered then to me.

"I will keep ringing you up to enquire about you. Maybe some day we will meet again…I will come to Mumbai…I…I will really miss you," I heard Manu say even though I had moved thirty feet from him and the train had also begun to move slowly.

"Take care," she replied and the train zoomed off. I kept holding Manu this time around as I did not want him to embark on another chase-and-catch spree.

"Shall we leave now, you lucky ass?" I said pointedly with poison spewing from each word that I uttered.

"I am sorry, dude. You had to suffer because of me, but don't worry…I will make it up to you some day. Let's get into the next train going back to Jaipur. It is supposed to leave at 5:30 from this station," he said.

"How...one second...how do you know that? We were not supposed to be here…we were supposed to get down at Sanganer…how come that you know about the timings of the trains that leave from here?" I must have been a fool not to have understood this till now. Manu knew all about the trains passing through Sanganer and also the exact time intervals and distance between the stations. I should have realised this earlier. Now I understood how calmly he had shown me two tickets on the Mumbai-bound train but which were for undertaking the journey till Sawai Madhopur. Now I realised why he looked so calm and nonplussed, while I fretted and fumed.

"You fucking asshole...it was all planned, wasn't it?" I asked, landing a solid slap on the back of his head. He simply smiled in response. My anger had started to lose its sting by now and I had begun to feel considerably calm and cool. The knowledge that I had proved helpful when he needed me began to seep into my mind. How else could I have consoled my wildly thumping heart!

The train we were supposed to board was a local train with only general class coaches. Manu had already bought the tickets at Jaipur and as luck would have it, the train was late. It started from the station only at 6:30 and that too on a journey which could never be forgotten. People were packed inside the coach like sardines and there were no reserved seats for anyone. All kinds of smells bordering on stench emitted from every corner and some passengers on the upper berths had placed their shoes against the grill of the fans installed on the ceiling and these were spreading the not-so pleasing stench everywhere. I had never encountered such a scene ever in my life. The train moved at a snail's pace and halted at almost every possible station that fell on the route. I puked more than once through the window and my whole body was wet with perspiration. All along the journey I kept on cursing Manu and he in reply, continued to grin back annoyingly. He didn't seem a wee bit bothered about the environs. He was so lost in love, you see.

It was only at 10:30 that we reached the Durgapura Railway Station. I reached home at around 11:00 p.m. It was on the way back home from the station that he chose to apologise to me, making me respond with, "It is okay" every time. I somehow avoided all the questions that were asked at home. I was too tired to answer them. Studying was the last thing that I wished to do in the frame of mind that I was. I was damn tired and the unexpected trip had caught me unawares and spoilt my plans for sure. As I flopped down on my bed that night, the events of the day kept on reappearing in front of my eyes. Manu had got what he wanted but I observed that my mind kept on going back to thoughts about Noopur a lot more all of a sudden. I wondered if I had actually begun to feel something special for her. Was it a genuine feeling or could it be something that was temporary? I wondered if she was to go away, would I also feel the same way as Manu had done for Carol? Did I really care that much about her? Was it too early to feel anything at all for her? I was just a kid...no?

I had no answers for the questions, though I was tired and far from my normal spirits. Anyway, I slept with a smile on my face.

After all it is said that *love is just a beginning towards the state of bewilderment!*

5

And I Talked…

It had almost been a week since I had undertaken that horrendous train ride with Manu. Maybe it wasn't horrendous for him as I could see that he seemed in a euphoric state of mind since the day he had seen her off. Also it was more than a hundred times since I had narrated the day's event in detail to Rahul, who had heard it many times from my lips and still not had enough of it. He was still miffed over the fact that he was not present when all this took place. I was, as expected, enjoying elaborating on it on every possible opportunity that I got, though I tried to drive home the point that he was lucky to escape from the ordeal that I had to go through. This story spread soon like wild fire and by the end of it, many more people came to know of it than could ever be imagined. Aniket was equally interested in knowing the sequence of events as they had occurred and both he and Parv never seemed satisfied despite hearing it again and again.

Talking of Parv, I had not yet recovered from the kiss that he had planted on my cheeks and my anger towards him not so far had evaporated. Kisses can be very hard to forget, especially if they are from one guy to another and this I had learned in one single bike ride, thanks to him!

It was almost September and that meant the first terminal exams were round the corner. I was still looking for opportunities to talk to her since that train ride but did not have that courage to go and say even a 'hello' to her. The reason was that my eagerness to talk to her had begun to dwindle due to the combined effect of the forthcoming school exams as well as the coaching review tests. Both were weighing heavy on my mind. I actually did not care much about the school exams but I was more concerned about the review tests. I wanted to ensure that my rank would continue to improve. I had not prepared yet for the review tests as the school exams ensured that I would not have any time to spare for that.

"I think I have screwed it," I told Aniket after the chemistry exam.

"Despite screwing everything around, you still score good marks buddy, so do not worry," Aniket replied.

"But I haven't written anything in the paper worth mentioning and that is why I am worried. I was sure of these review tests making my life a mess...and they have done it finally. In chemistry I have screwed for sure this time," I said, feeling dejected. It was just a day before the chemistry exam that the review tests had taken place. I had not found even a minute to go through the chemistry book. It wasn't as though the courses at the school and the coaching class were different. On the contrary, it had helped me a lot with the school exams. But the truth remained that I was pretty poor in chemistry, both at school and at the coaching class. I had more often than not faced negative marks in chemistry at the coaching, so it was undoubtedly a relief to learn that there was no system of negative marking in the school exams.

"Thank God, finally the exams have got over," Rahul said, joining Aniket and me as we stood on the basketball court, busy discussing the test paper.

"Arori says he has screwed it and do you think we can believe it?" Aniket turned to ask Rahul.

"I have...believe me," I said.

"I know he must have done it for sure…even Manu is hiding his face. He has screwed his biology paper. Both of them were so happily riding on the train to Mumbai a few days back, I wouldn't be surprised if they both wrote the same story in the exams also. I know it because I have been subjected to hearing that story almost a hundred times," Rahul said, hi-fiving Aniket.

"Add my hundred times too. This time I have to believe him," Aniket replied laughingly.

"Very funny! Damn it...and it is chemistry," I said.

"Yeah…we all know your love for chemistry and don't worry, I know you have left quite an impact on Mr. Chaturvedi's mind. He won't fail you."

"Yeah…with that kind of impression, I can only hope for it to work. That's my only chance."

Strangely enough, the chemistry papers were checked in a couple of days and as expected, I had flunked. Sometime later it struck me that there was something dubious about the marks. I had scored 21 marks out of 70, which meant that I was about 7 marks short from the passing marks. What struck me as strange was that the mark-sheet had some overwriting done on my marks and it seemed as if the total of 31 had been intentionally changed to 21. I knew I was going to flunk but the overwriting needed clarification for sure.

"Excuse me, sir, I would like to see my answer sheet," I went and said to Mr. Chaturvedi.

"Why? Do you think I haven't checked your paper properly? I am not showing anyone the paper. The marks that have been given are final," he replied firmly.

"Sir…but I think there is some mistake somewhere. I am saying this because there is some overwriting on the mark sheet. I think I had scored 31 but by mistake, someone has changed the marks to 21. I will be highly obliged if you could please check this out, sir," I begged, trying to be as respectful as possible.

"I told you I am not re-checking anything. The marks that are given on the mark sheet are final. You are hardly present in school and yet you expect good marks? Get lost from here," he screamed (literally), paying no heed to my plea. He threw a look of disgust at my face when saying it all.

I could not stand there any longer. I knew no matter what I did, he would not budge from his stand. Feeling completely disheartened, I went and sat down on my chair. I was still feeling bad at not having made the grade and the overwriting had left me more irritated. Aniket had remained silent all this while, probably at not getting good marks himself though he had managed to pass.

"So you have finally flunked?" Manu asked as he entered the class, along with Rahul. Mr. Chaturvedi had left the classroom to go to the staff room.

"Chaturvedi showed his true colours. I did not expect him to fail Aadi. There is even some overwriting on the mark sheet. I am sure there is something wrong somewhere," said Aniket to Manu.

"Why don't you go and check it out…?" asked Rahul.

"No use…," I said with a dejected look.

"Don't worry…I know you will clear the supplementary for sure and that too with good marks. Then he will realise what a big blunder he has committed by failing you…don't worry at all," Rahul said.

"I am not worried…It is simply this that I will not feel great at having to give some fucking supplementary exam all alone."

"Arori…Parv has also failed. You will always have his company," Aniket replied, smiling naughtily as if he was giving the greatest news of his lifetime to me.

"Yeah…you can always come to me and enjoy the pleasure of my company, *sahib,*" Parv said, giving again that irritating grin of his. This guy was surely going to get killed by me some day. I ignored his comment as I did not want to remember that stinky, salivary kiss of his. I avoided him therefore.

"Oye…she has flunked too. I had seen her name in the mark sheet. She got 21 only; same as you," Aniket said again.

"Is this the reason for which I should be happy? Both she and I have flunked and I should be feeling glad about that?" I asked.

"This is your official licence to talk to her. Don't you understand this simple thing?" Manu asked.

"Yeah man, you don't want to wait like Manu, do you?" Rahul quizzed.

"I don't know…I am not thinking about that right now. I have to clear the supplementary first," I replied, without looking into their eyes.

"You will remain an ass forever. The supplementary exams are after a month and there are no review tests clashing with it, so stop making such a hue and cry about it," Aniket told me without mincing any words.

"But…." I was interrupted in between.

"Let's meet up tonight somewhere and then we will plan up about it. Is it okay now?" Rahul said, looking towards me.

It wasn't a request from him; it was just a genuine decision. I silently nodded in agreement.

"Yeah…and we will not go to Nahargarh today," Parv added. Nobody had asked him to air his views, but the black hole that he was, how could he ever spare us?

That evening, after my coaching class, we all met at the Café Coffee Day at Gaurav Towers. It was the oldest mall in Jaipur and a pioneer in the urban development of the city. This place was only a-five minute drive away from the coaching institute and was considered the most happening place in the city. People from outside used to argue that it was not that sophisticated or classy but the fact remained that for students like us, who invariably led a hand to mouth existence by way of cash, it was the best place to chill out.

"I still cannot believe Chaturvedi actually did that. He could not have done it…I suspect there's someone else's hand involved in it. Maybe somebody has played a prank on you," said Aniket. We all had not even exchanged 'hellos' and here he was talking about my marks, meaning that it was uppermost in his mind. He must have been thinking only about this since the time he had seen the mark sheet.

"We will talk about this later; right now our purpose is different and it is on top of our priority list," Rahul remarked to Aniket. Manu was standing near the counter to place the order. I hated him placing the order because whenever he did so, we had to eat everything on the menu that had chocolate in it. I liked the flavour of chocolate but not excess of it. So my attention was less on what they were talking but more on what Manu was up to.

"Manu, don't order the choco fudge this time…it was pathetic the last time we ate it," I squealed. Everyone else present in the room turned to glance at me. I pretended as if I had done nothing wrong by talking loudly.

"Did you hear what I said?" Rahul asked.

"Yes…I did. I hope Manu doesn't get that choco fudge. It is a tongue-piercer when it comes to taste," I replied, deliberately avoiding the topic of discussion.

"You are going to talk to her today, Arori…we have everything planned," Aniket said, holding me by my hand and shaking me tightly as if to awaken me into action.

"What? Are you crazy? I am not talking to her. What will I say to her? Hello…I am a classmate of yours and one whom you don't know…We haven't talked ever with each other, but I like you and that's why I am happy that you flunked just as I did. So this gives me an opportunity to hook up to you…and we will be happy ever after! You want me to say this and get my ass fucked? No way, dude…I have some sense," I said angrily. I did not realise that I was squeaking at a pitch higher than normal and many eyeballs were focused on me. Manu reached us meanwhile with his tray loaded with almost everything that was there on the menu. I noticed there was that awful choco fudge right in the middle of the tray.

"And see…now this idiot has got that choco fudge too...," I said, complaining loudly.

"Shut up, Aadi…one more word and I will beat your ass up….you are calling her tonight right in front of us all. We are not asking you to talk for an hour or anything….just give a bloody call on the pretext of asking her for some notes and stuff. That's all you have to do!" Rahul said between his clenched teeth so that nobody else around would hear his words.

"Yeah….otherwise one day she will go away and then, don't expect me to give you company on some stupid train ride," Manu said in a bantering tone. Nobody laughed. He just gave a self-satisfactory grin and continued sipping his stupid choco frappe.

"Parv has managed to get her number too," Aniket said confidently.

"It's 98……" Parv began telling me the number while drawing close to hold my hand.

"Fuck you…why do you keep getting close to me, weirdo?" I screamed angrily, pushing his hand back with disgust. This time nobody looked at me. Everyone had possibly become used to hearing my screeches by now. He pulled away his hand immediately, laughing loudly. Manu, Aniket and Rahul laughed along with him.

"Guys, I am really in no fit state to do as you desire. I haven't thought about talking to her yet. I will not be able to utter a word to her. Everything will be spoiled…I am sure! Moreover, I still have the Damocles sword about the supplementary exam hanging over my head. Please try to understand my situation," I begged.

"You always spoil every plan, man…here we all were so excited. Are you serious that you won't do it?" Rahul asked, looking dejected.

"I can't do it right now," I said, looking away from him.

"Okay…it's your say after all. But at least, take down her number. You can use it later some day," said Aniket. Parv made me save the number in my cell phone. I saved it simply to put an end to the issue. I was aware that I would never get down to using it. I did want to talk to her but only when I felt up to it and considered it a right moment to do so. They all were forcing me to do something for which I was hardly prepared, mentally or physically.

We all just sat talking about this and that and I could see the excitement that had been palpable earlier was missing since

I refused to talk to Noopur. Meanwhile I was struggling to swallow Manu's all-chocolate-loaded order though I could see him relishing and enjoying what all lay in front of him. We all got ready to leave for our respective homes when my cell phone rang. The caller's name flashed in large fonts on the LCD screen.

"Now, who the hell is playing some dirty trick on me?" I asked, screeching again.

"Why, what has happened?" they all asked in one voice.

"This...." I said and showed them the name flashing on my mobile. It was Noopur. Everyone looked shocked.

"Pick it up," Rahul said.

I was in two minds about picking up the phone but noticing all eyes looking at me in anticipation, I felt I had no other course of action except to pick up the call. Could someone be playing a prank on me? I looked at them, one by one, but they did not seem to be good actors.

"Hello!" It was a female voice at the other end.

"Hello!" I replied.

"Can I speak to Aadvitya please? It's Noopur here," she said. I felt blood surge through my veins as if some electric current had been passed through my body. Oh my God, it was her...wanting to talk to me. I dropped down heavily on the couch. The voice had sounded so amazing now. I had heard so many females over the phone but this one sounded so different. My name had never sounded so sweet. I felt all my senses grow numb, the world go in a tizzy and my head swim in a daze. Could it be that I was dreaming?

"Aaahhhnnn...." I shrieked because Manu was shaking me violently.

"Is it her?" he was whispering in my ear.

"What? Hello?" she began to ask again.

"Aaa…ya...i…it…it's Aadvitya here," I said, speaking more in my normal tone.

"Is it her?" Now it was Rahul's turn to whisper. I noticed Aniket and Parv looking with their eyeballs falling out of their sockets. I gestured to them to keep quiet.

"Hi…yeah…actually I just called up to ask you for some help," she said.

"Yeah…yeah...," I replied. I could not think of anything else to say. By now all of them had realised to whom I was talking. Aniket was giving me a mouthful of abuses and Manu had ordered for another chocolate stuff.

"Act… actually, I haven't scored great marks in chemistry this time around...you are going to these coaching classes and all…I was wondering if you could help me with your notes and stuff?" she asked in the sweetest possible tone.

"Yeah…" I replied. I received a slap on my back from Aniket. "Say something doggie..." he whispered.

"Okay…thanks then…goodbye," she said.

"Yeah…yeah," I repeated again as she put down the phone. This time I received a slap on the back of my head but from Rahul as I hung up.

"Do you know you did not utter a word to her? You let go of such a valuable opportunity, you dumbhead," said Rahul. I noticed Aniket nod in affirmation. Parv was giving that same ugly smile of his. Manu loved his chocolate milkshake more than anything else.

"The moment that call came I ordered my milkshake. The bill is being footed by Aadi today. First conversation with her, after all!" Manu said, drawing his attention away from his chocolate shake. A few drops dripped on the floor from his mouth as he said the words, but he seemed unconcerned. It was free, after all.

"Pay 500 bucks now for uttering nothing but a few yeahs, yeahs on the phone. Stupid…you seriously need to be clobbered on your head to make you come to your senses," Rahul said as I footed the bill. I did not care for what he was saying. Till now the thought of giving the supplementary examination had been uppermost in my mind but now it had been replaced with thoughts about her. We moved out of the café but my mind was in the clouds. Her every word was echoing in my mind again and again. Rahul, Aniket and Parv were walking in front of me, while Manu was still sipping the last drops of his chocolate shake, making weird noises with the straw.

"Huh, he really spoilt it all…what was the use of his talking to her today?" I heard Aniket say as I followed behind.

I just said to myself, 'At least I talked…'

6

Did it Signify a Beginning for Me?

'Dis is Jai here. Stay away 4m Neha... els u will repent big tym' – Aniket showed me this message that he had received on his cell phone that night. He had mentioned this to me already over the phone but I had told him to ignore it as a false threat. People do love playing pranks at times. He had asked me to reach early that day at the school and for his satisfaction, I had followed his instructions. Rahul and Manu too had arrived early. Obviously, Aniket had discussed the issue with them too. Parv was nowhere to be seen though I heaved a sigh of relief to see him missing from the scene. Aniket, as expected, was fuming with anger at the message he had received.

"Once...only once I have to get to know who that bastard is and I will get the shit out of him," said Aniket, fuming through his nose. His eyes had become blood shot and it wasn't the first time that we had seen him in such a state. There had been times earlier also when we had seen him go crazy if someone said something about Neha. He never spared that person and made sure to drive the hell out of him. Even I had to bear his brunt once while playing volleyball at the school grounds. I remarked something in good humour but he took it otherwise and what followed was a volley of abuses from him. It was another thing that he was the first person to come and apologise later to me. I found his behaviour quite strange but I had refrained from saying something to him.

"Calm down, man…just call back that number and ask… what is his name? Yeah…Jai. Ask him what is his freaking problem?" Rahul said. That suggestion however went in vain. Whoever had sent that SMS had used a lot of brains in sending the message through the internet that enabled him to keep his identity hidden. In those days, the free SMS sites were not as popular as they are today. That person called Jai had used the Rediff messenger service to send the text. The messenger allowed the user to send a maximum of three SMS a day to a particular receiving number until the receiver replied back on the same id. If the receiver did not reply to any of the messages, then no more messages could be sent on the receiver's number on that particular day. The id used in this case was 'jai_malothra@rediff.com' where I found the spelling of Malhotra quite ambiguous as no acquaintance of mine with that name spelled it as Malothra. So obviously the aim of the caller was to hide his identity from me. This way he could avoid getting caught.

"Where is Parv today? I can't see him anywhere?" I asked.

"I told him what had happened. He is checking out if we can trace the message on the internet. I told you before also that he is good at these things," explained Aniket very slowly.

"Huh, that black hole wants to behave like James Bond now. Bloody lunatic," I muttered.

"Arori...that's rude! He is at least trying to help me out," said Aniket without even a hint of a smile on his face. I knew he was tense.

"Whatever!" I replied in a hushed voice. Aniket's cell phone rang meanwhile and we noticed that we still had some time left before joining our classes. So it was safe to pick up the phone inside the school. He went to a corner to talk while Manu, Rahul and I began to figure out as to who could be suspected of sending such a message. We were actually not taking it that seriously as we felt it was some sort of a prank. Manu thought it could be Ananya, the specky with a messed up hairstyle, and one who was always lost in something or the other. Manu's reason for suspecting her was that even in movies, the least suspicious characters turned out to be the real culprits in the end. So his view was that we should not waste time on others but try to apprehend the innocents first. His view no doubt amounted to less of logic and more to surmise.

"Guys...I have got to go...Parv is waiting for me outside. He is saying that he has succeeded in tracing the IP address of the PC from which the message was sent. School hasn't started yet...I can get out easily...I am leaving," said Aniket, walking away briskly.

"Dude, you can surely go once the school gets over. What's the hurry? Come on, relax! If someone gets to know that you have bunked, you will be in serious trouble," warned Manu.

"Yeah," Rahul and I spoke out simultaneously.

"I can't let that rascal escape with this," he said, picking up his school bag and running out of the class. As expected, no one stopped him at the school gate. From the classroom window, I saw him and Parv zoom away on the latter's bike.

"It seems like your James Bond is bound to do some wonders! C'mon Aadi, the guy isn't that bad," Rahul said.

"Yeah...he isn't that bad as long as he doesn't kiss you. I have felt that saliva floating on my cheeks...my pretty cheeks...they still stink!" I replied.

"Thank your God it was only on your cheeks. It could have been worse, you know," Manu said, smiling cheekily at me.

"Fuck off," I said, pushing them out of the classroom.

Strangely enough, not many students had come to the school that day. Aniket had already bunked the class with Parv, while Rahul and Manu were in the other section. I knew it was going to be tough to pass time. I wasn't worried about the message frankly as I felt that Aniket was making a mountain out of a molehill. The first lecture after the assembly was as usual on chemistry. Even though I knew I had to appear for the supplementary exam, I slept during the entire lecture without any fear as I was seated on the last bench. Curiously, Mr. Chaturvedi did not even bother to look at me during the entire lecture. The next subject was physics during which too I managed to while away my time. The next two lectures were devoted to physical education where I knew that my luck would not hold out for very long. I decided not to take a chance as there were only a few students present in the class and the teacher decided to go for the practicals. Actually, physical education was an elective subject for us. We had to choose between computer science and physical education and we had chosen the latter as it was considered to be a cakewalk. This increased my chances of getting a higher percentage in the Boards without wasting too much of sweat.

In the initial phase of my life, I had been pretty active in sports but as I grew older and acquired a few extra ounces on my belly, my flexibility and interest compelled me to move away from things that required the use of body parts. Having slept quietly during the earlier two lectures, I was in no mood to go outside and sweat uselessly. I knew that making an excuse wouldn't help but knowing there was no other way to escape from the ordeal, I decided to give it a try. I was frightened of the stick he held in his hand but still I went to his desk with a pale-looking face to ask innocently if I could be excused from attending the class. My acting skills were not that bad maybe, as I had thought. I was simply allowed to stay back in class and carry on sleeping from where I had left earlier. I wonder if I had asked God for the whole world that day, he would have granted that too!

I straightaway went back to my bench and kept my head down on the table for the first half an hour or so. I had to pretend I was feeling under weather, so I had to keep my head down. Not once did I raise my head up for the entire two lectures. It was only when the first bell rang that I opened my eyes to look around me and what I saw was something out of my imagination. There was not a single soul in the classroom except me and her. She was seated near the window on the opposite corner of the classroom, busy doing some assignments. After her phone call that evening, we had talked only once again and that too on phone where I had stuttered and stammered as always. Possibly realising that I was of no help, she was copying down notes from somebody's notebook. I noticed her pen moving at a fast speed – so fast as if she was participating in a race with someone. All she seemed to lack was a red Ferrari. She was leaning down on the desk while writing and I couldn't prevent myself from marvelling at the beauty of the hair flicks that covered her side face. The bright sunshine falling from the window imparted an ethereal glow to her face, making her face look as if she had just emerged from the wrapper of the white Dove soap. In between I noticed her pushing her hair away as they came to fall on her face every now and then. I was trying to keep my eyes away but couldn't help myself from staring at her. It was then that I could understand what must have been the plight of Sage Vishwamitra when Menaka was sent by Lord Indra to entice him and break his penance. Also, it was then I realised that if you are a male, you are bound to get attracted to a female and lose your senses. I knew history was being repeated once again because I was starting to lose my senses to this beauty. I realised now how beautiful she was and if given a chance, I could have continued to stare at her till eternity.

I very reluctantly put my head down once again on the table as I felt I should not look at her any further. I closed my eyes very tightly, so that I would not be tempted to stare at her again. I tried to concentrate on things other than her, but to no avail. I thought about the strawberry custard that I loved eating once I reached home; I thought about how the gears of my bike changed as I pressed the clutch; I thought about the beautiful curves of the woman from the recent porn film I had watched till 4 o'clock in the morning while everyone else slept. On the contrary, I found that my mind started to work in the wrong direction, imagining all kinds of impossible things.

With my head down, I tried to recapture the look I had seen when my head was up and slyly stealing glances at her. Very slowly I raised my head and looked towards her. She was still busy writing something and looking gorgeous as ever. I hurriedly searched for something in my school bag and fished out a week-old slab of chocolate given to me by a classmate on his birthday and due to boredom with chocolates, I had kept it inside my bag to eat it some other day. It had melted to the core and its wrapper had lost that sheen of a fresh buy, yet I said, 'Thank God!'

It did not take me a second even to think and then move. I promptly got up from my seat and went and stood near her bench, but only after gulping some water from my bottle and adjusting my hair. She was still deeply engrossed in completing her assignment and her pen was moving fast at a frantic pace. She did not seem to notice me.

"Noopur," I said softly in order not to shock her out of her wits. But she did not hear me. She was deeply entrenched in her task and completely oblivious of the world around her. I thought that maybe I had spoken her name in too low a volume. So I repeated again, "Noopur," slightly adjusting my volume regulator. She moved this time and looked up straight into my eyes. This was the first time I got to lock my eyes with hers. Her eyes were lined with black kohl and the fairness of her skin made the kohl look darker still. I looked down to stare at her legs. They were equally beautiful and spotless, though pretty irrelevant, I knew!

"Please accept this chocolate from me," I said. How dumb could I be! Donkey! Bummer! I knew I had got it wrong. I could not find anything else to say. I could have tried some other sophisticated way of saying it but on seeing her face to face, my mind refused to function. The multi-tasking processor had become an age-old Pentium, maybe.

"Why?" she asked in an innocent voice. At least she could have said something more than just to ask a 'why', or better still, she could have accepted the chocolate straightaway.

My heart had begun to thud loudly across my ribs as if ready to burst out of its encasing. It did not require even a stethoscope to hear how it was pounding.

"Because that's for you," I said stupidly, while cursing myself within my heart of hearts. I had made a terrible mess of the golden opportunity that had come my way. She was still looking into my eyes with amazement, as I stood seeing all my hopes go down the drain. I looked at her hand which was gripping the pen tightly. It looked so soft and pretty. I was tempted to hold the hand in my hands and kiss it. A minute or two of silence elapsed before she extended her hand and took the chocolate from my hand. In the process, her hand touched mine and a shudder went right through my spine. I felt as if I had touched silk or velvet. She gave me a crooked smile and blushed. I wondered if there was anything left to add to her beauty. I wanted to stay there and keep looking at her face forever. Her enchanting smile took my breath away. I did not say anything further to her; in any case I was in no condition to say anything. The recess bell rang and I knew staying there any longer was fraught with innumerable dangers. I slowly want back to my bench with a shocked expression on my face. On the way I collided into a couple of empty desks, bruising my knee in the process. My eyes were not seeing anything; my legs were taking me nowhere and my ears were not hearing anything. I just went and sat back on my bench with disbelief writ large on my face. I did not have the guts to even turn and look at her to check if she was smiling at my clumsiness…

It has been very rightly said that *love is the seventh sense that numbs all the other six senses!*

7

Could We be Friends?

A number of incidents occurred in the days that followed. Parv and Aniket could not identify who it was to send the anonymous message from the internet, though they had succeeded in locating the site from which it had come. Parv told me the following points while trying to explain the fundamentals of IP addresses:

- No more messages could follow after that initial message (which meant peace for all of us)
- I had become freer with Noopur after the chocolate encounter though our talks were restricted to once a week over the phone or when running into each other at school. (I don't know the reason for it being so)
- My supplementary exam had drawn nearer (which meant I had to become prey to still more stern looks from Mr. Chaturvedi in the classroom)
- I was in love about which I was still not fully sure yet

With the exception of Manu, we all had decid to go to Parv's hostel that evening. Manu had deliberately chosen to stay away as he wanted to talk surreptitiously to Carol over the phone. I had read somewhere that you cannot have love and friends together. This wasn't exactly the case but the guy had certainly undergone a sea change since being struck by Cupid's arrow.

In all we were only three persons – Aniket, Rahul and I at Parv's hostel after sunset that day. Expectedly, I wasn't keen on setting foot inside the place but since Parv was nothing else but good in Aniket's eyes, I too had to accept him. In any case, Aniket seemed to be a big fan of hostel life. I was more of a homely guy for whom the mere thought of living away from parents and home used to give me the creeps. I had decided to stay back forever at Jaipur at home. Aniket's case was different for he wasn't bothered about staying away from home and living all alone. The only point he never failed to drive home was that he received unlimited freedom by staying away from home. There had been times when I had been forced to hear about his experiences with booze, cigarettes and sex. Well, sex was undoubtedly a tempting proposition but the fear of leaving home and all the related comforts always held sway. It was this fascination for limitless freedom that had made Parv occupy the pride of place in Aniket's heart. What Aniket could only dream about, Parv was probably able to live to the core!

The hostel was just a couple of kilometres away from my place. I had nothing to do with whatever went on in the hostel. Since the school did not have its own hostel, this place had been rented by a majority of the students coming from outside Jaipur to study, due to its proximity to the school campus. I neither had any experience with the place nor was I ever bothered about its existence. However, the fact that Parv stayed here made me presume that the place could be nothing short of a brothel (maybe a gay brothel).

"Oh *sahib*! I had been expecting you," Parv said, leaping forward to hug me as soon as he saw us ascend the stairs to his block. Anticipating his action, I quickly pushed Aniket ahead of me so that I would not have to tolerate his hug.

"Yo buddy! We had to be here," Aniket said, equalling him in the intensity of their mutual greetings. I had full sympathy for Aniket. Parv's room was on the second floor with five more single-occupant rooms. The rooms were commonly attached to a large area that served both as a dining hall and a television lounge. The place wore a deserted look with no human activity visible.

"The crowd doesn't seem to be here today," I said, while following Rahul and Aniket into Parv's room through the hall. Rahul, to my surprise, was quite subdued that day as he held on to his mobile like a precious treasure.

"*Sahib,* we always make sure you get to meet the right people only," he said, looking at me and grinning wickedly through his saliva-dripping mouth. I immediately looked away to avoid puking. He opened the door of the room and I saw a strong smell emanate from the room in which sat Ayush Malhaar (yeah...the last name sounds weird) surrounded by three recently opened Vodka bottles. It was easy to get booze in Jaipur. The government had found it feasible to collect revenue this way. As a result, Jaipur was now blessed with licensed liquor shops at almost every corner and despite the initial protests, the move was welcomed by the young crowd.

"You got to be kidding me! Is this for real?" asked Aniket, sitting down on the floor along with Ayush, who was beating his large tummy with his hands. He was from our batch but seldom attended classes as he was preparing for his medical entrance exams.

I was told that his Dad owned the largest hospital at Ajmer and thus wanted the son to follow in his footsteps. In any case, the son looked like a rich, fat ass with three bellies (actually it was one belly but the vastness and the circumference of his tummy kept us guessing about the number).

"You aren't joining in *sahib?*" Parv asked me as he sat down on the floor. Frankly I had yet to develop a liking for alcohol and it was at moments like these that I always felt out of place. I had to make up an excuse fast enough!

"I would like to watch some television first," I said and left the room.

"Me too!" Rahul followed behind me.

I switched on the TV and sat down on the couch placed right in front of the television set. Rahul sat down next to me. I don't remember if I talked much that day but I remember Rahul being annoyingly busy with his cell phone while the others were preoccupied with their booze. Whenever we would launch on a discussion, he would receive an SMS on his cell phone and get occupied with replying to it. Though I was curious to know whom he was messaging, I avoided asking him. I hadn't seen him so much involved with his cell ever. Nobody else had noticed this sudden development but I had, from one corner of my eye stationed at his actions.

"Where can I have access to the internet here?" Rahul asked me all of a sudden. I gestured with my hands to convey I had no idea.

"I need it urgently," he said frantically, moving to the room where the rest of the gang was seated. My reply remained where it belonged: inside my mouth!

Parv showed him the way. First, it was the cell phone and then, the sudden need for the internet. My curiosity reached an all time high on seeing the desperate look on his face. I was keen to know why he needed the internet so urgently. Though I focused my eyes on the television screen, my ears were parked at what he was saying. Meanwhile in the adjoining room, I could sense that booze had started to show its effect as I could hear a flood of abuses floating out.

Gggrrrrrrrrrrrr...I heard the vibrations. It was Rahul's mobile phone that was vibrating. He had left it behind on the couch before leaving the place. The phone conveyed that an SMS was being received. This was my opportunity to pick up the mobile and raise the volume of the television. The mobile was on the lock code. I entered Rahul's number 7985, but it did not work. Then I entered the digits 1607, which stood for his date of birth. Even then it failed to work. I tried a couple of other numbers that I could think of, but none worked. Suddenly the cell phone began to ring. I picked it up but it was blocked. I was tempted to throw back the mobile on the couch but the desire to know what Rahul was up to, made my mind strike on a valuable idea. I entered the digits 5683 which corresponded to the word LOVE in T9 in the cell phone. Eureka, it worked. The soft key on the left was giving me the option to read the message. I peeped into the adjoining room and saw Ayush rolling on the floor with Aniket and Parv on top of him. I had heard that booze did that to some people. I noticed empty bottles littering the floor. Without delaying any further, I pressed the key to read the SMS. It read as follows:

"Wher r u mah huny? M w8in..."

I scrolled down to see the sender's name and was shocked to see Mallya on it. Yeah, the same Mallya who was from the commerce section and on whom Rahul had a huge crush. But I had heard that he had never talked to her. Looking at that SMS on the screen did not shock me as much as it troubled me. I immediately checked the other messages on the inbox.

"Awww baby! I hv ben misin u…luv u!"

"U dint brng mah present? How rude!"

It was all from Mallya. From the first message in the inbox to the last message, it was all her. Of course, there were a couple of cheap adult forwards from my number too but they seemed negligible in front of the messages from Mallya's cell. This actually meant that it was not a recent development but had been going on for quite some time. I placed the phone back on the couch and glanced at the drunkards. Aniket was trying to light a cigarette. It seemed he was bent on making the most of the freedom that he had got that day. But I was frantic to reach back home. My eyes went towards Ayush's belly, which was still vibrating as he and Parv were up to something repulsive. My mind went to Rahul who could have told us about his affair. I mean none of us was keeping any secret within us. Whatever happened was equally shared amongst us. I wondered why Rahul was being so secretive about his affair? What was wrong in telling us? He would have been subjected to some teasing, some jesting and that's all. What else!

My thinking process came to a sudden halt when I heard the sound of loud laughter (possibly Ravana, the king of Lanka must have laughed like this in front of Rama as narrated in our mythology). Ayush was kneeling down on the ground while Aniket and Parv were ready to force their abdominal side into his ass. I was relieved to find that they at least had their clothes on. It was again Ayush's tummy which was bearing the brunt of the force of gravity and I wondered whether it was his mouth or his stomach that was making strange sounds. On seeing me, all of them halted suddenly and sat back on the floor, away from each other. Alcohol could really do unpredictable things. Everyone reacts so differently to it. My mind went into the thinking mode again…

Rahul had a girl friend now, Manu got one a few weeks back (yeah...sort of), Aniket had one since he was born (or at an age when I did not even know that there were two different sexes in this world); it was only I who did not have any (apart from Parv, of course).

The door opened in a flash and Rahul entered the hall, looking rather relaxed. I left my thought process midway and shouted, "Bastard, I need to speak to you." Maybe I was waiting for this moment only.

One message received

Someone's cell phone buzzed and Rahul immediately picked up his cell, but only after throwing a meaningful stare at me. His cell couldn't have rung. It was on the vibration mode, I remembered. I was about to ask him as to what was being cooked when suddenly Aniket came out from the next room and pushed the giant screen of his cell phone straight into my face. I banged my forehead in frustration on seeing what was written on the screen. The call was from Jai…

* * * * *

I knew Aniket was still thinking about that message while we were on our way back home from Ayush's hospital that night. He had drunk too much and was deep in depression. It had been a lethal combination. And seeing the way he was driving, I was reminded of a mad elephant gone amok. The SMS was from the same id that had been used earlier. It said the same thing that the previous SMS had done but with minor additions.

Aniket was advised to stay away from Neha and threatened that if he did not do so, then the next SMS would be delivered to his Dad's number. To add authenticity to the message, the SMS also mentioned his Dad's cell number. Certainly such a threat was bound to affect any normal human being's mental composure (and here he was in a drunken state). It was another matter that it was I who was gasping for breath as he drove my bike at a reckless pace.

"……?" Aniket said something.

"What?" I yelled. The bike's pace was making it impossible for me to hear anything apart from the sound of the air. He suddenly halted the bike without any warning and my chest bumped into his back. I did not give any reaction.

"Who is doing this to me?" he asked bluntly, looking back at me.

"It's just an SMS…don't be so tense," I said, getting down from the bike. I was worried, to tell the truth, despite putting on such a brave front. But I did not wish to add to his worries.

"Only Manu wasn't there when the message came. I can bet my head, it is someone from among us."

"Are you crazy? It can't be Manu…I am sure of that guy," I said with conviction.

"And I am sure of Parv and you," he said, trying to convey something meaningful.

"What do you want to say? Didn't you notice it when Rahul went out in quest of the internet?" I said, desperately trying to ignore the stench of the alcohol lingering in the air. These cheap mints in the market proved to be of no use.

My mind was still coming to terms with the possibilities when he added, "Even the IP address that Parv traced belongs to some PC on V.T. Road. From amongst us, only Rahul lives there."

I did not look towards him. I simply pushed him on to the pillion and went and sat down on the front seat. I didn't say anything to him and in any case he wasn't bothered about my reaction. All I knew was that a big storm was awaiting us all in the coming days….

8

From Sheer Darkness, I Conquer Chemistry

"Sssssshhhhhhhhhh...don't make a noise," he said.

"You are scaring me. I am not doing anything," I replied into the darkness, holding the dim torch in my hand.

I remember I had only two nights before the supplementary exam was to start. I was still battling hard to prevent my eyes from closing shut. The textbook published by NCERT with chemistry written on it in bold letters was still in my hands while Jagjit Singh's *ghazals* played on my computer's speakers. It had been an hour since I had opened the page that explained the difference between a ketone and an aldehyde. It had taken me five minutes to understand the link between double-bonded oxygen with carbon and hydrogen in the respective cases. The rest 55 minutes were spent on scratching the boldly written word 'chemistry' on the book cover *('arrgghhh...how I hated chemistry!)*.

My thoughts were wandering from place to place as I kept on scribbling my pen over the title *'Chemistry'* on the book. Just then I heard the sound of bikes coming from downstairs. In order to explain the reason for all this, let me tell you a bit about the background.

The black hole was screaming my name (*Oh, my God*)!

I went downstairs without thinking, though my mind had begun to somersault the moment it heard his voice. He was standing all alone and I wondered why Aniket hadn't accompanied him! What on earth did he want from me wondered.

"So, how are the preparations going on, *sahib*?" he asked, giving me such a filthy look to which I had become quite inured by now. He too had a supplementary exam, I wanted to tell him.

"Just started. Let's see," I replied, trying to sound disinterested.

He remained quiet, or maybe he did not. He said something but I did not bother to hear it. I didn't even bother to look at his face and preferred to look sideways on the murky street. I knew that a glance at his face would have made the night seem darker still. *(I knew I behaved like evil sometimes, but then who cared).* I looked at my watch a couple of times to convey that I wasn't interested in wasting time but he seemed to be unaware of my intention. *Dude! I ain't listening,* I wanted to scream.

"Just imagine…that will make the chemistry supplementary exam a joke." *Did I hear something?*

"What?" I asked foolishly.

"You have to come with me…I cannot do this alone. Chemistry will be tough to crack if we do it on our own, you know. Don't waste time now *Arori sahib;* come."

Arrgggghhhh….I so damn hated chemistry!

With that black hole in front of the school gate? Yuck!

I got off the bike as soon as we were at the school gate. I wanted to avoid being seen with him. It wasn't at all a great feeling to have his zombie hands in constant search for the tiniest bit of flesh on my body. A couple of guards were seated in the guard-room, sipping on to something hot (which I inferred was tea). I looked at the opposite end of the school gate. The single multipurpose shop that existed near the school was surprisingly shut that night. I still wasn't sure about the purpose of this visit. *Screw my ignorance for this guy,* I thought. I was still doubtful about my decision to accompany him.

"What next?" I asked as he parked the bike in the vacant plot adjacent to the school.

"Come…we are breaking through!" he replied, moving towards the gate. I stopped him in his track, pulling him roughly by his hand.

"You can't be serious, can you?"

"I wasn't joking!"

"I am not doing this, no…not at all," I said in a petrified tone at the very thought of entering the school premises without permission and doing something that meant crossing the limits. Certainly, this wasn't any joke being played.

"Don't do anything, *sahib*…there is nothing to do. Chemistry is easy for you, I know," he said seething with sarcasm! Pure sarcasm! The ultimate words by him pierced me right through my heart. I knew I was bad at chemistry as everyone else also knew. He was dragging me into something which my conscience did not permit to participate in. He started moving menacingly towards the school gate without bothering about me. I wondered how he was going to cross the guards. I had to make a decision urgently.

Arrggghhhhh…I so damn hated chemistry!

What was I thinking of doing?

"Sssssshhhhhhhhhh...don't make that noise," he said.

"You are scaring me. I am not doing anything," I shot back into the darkness, holding the dim torch in my trembling hand. I was still perturbed at the thought of being present in the school building at 8 in the night to search for papers that were to be in our hands two days later. My mind was debating whether I was doing the right thing or not. My brain was in a state of confusion and worry. I entered the school campus behind him, pretty aware of the consequences that were to follow if we were to get caught. Parv had handed over two crisp five hundred rupee notes to the guards without saying a word to them at the entrance. The badly-lit torch was handed to him in return for the money and the look that those two guards gave, made it seem that we were doing nothing unusual. Surely quite a few people were involved in this act – this was precisely the reason for my becoming more and more restless.

The school building, as expected, stood like a ghost house. Not a soul was to be seen anywhere. Not a single light illuminated the rooms and it was so pitch dark that I could not see even Parv except for his clothes (his body was of a similar tone as the darkness around). Every single room was bolted with a big silver lock that made entry next to impossible. I remembered that we had actually come to make a break through the locked doors. He was moving in front of me, continuously searching for something as I followed behind, unaware of his next move. It was the torch in my hand that made it possible for him to find his way ahead. We moved through the ground floor's corridors, passing our classroom on the way. I peeped in through the glass panes to check how the classrooms looked at night. All deserted. I imagined myself seated at the back bench of the second row with Rahul, Aniket, Manu and everyone else surrounding me. I gazed towards the now empty desk on which Noopur sat every day and it seemed more beautiful and tempting from the other benches. Foolish, I know!

"Come on, don't waste time and in any case, I can't see anything," Parv said slowly. I left my gazing midway and began to follow him up the stairs that led to the first floor. Except the way ahead, I wasn't able to see anything surrounding us. No notice-board seemed legible, no class bulletin was visible. It was just the blue tiled floor that I could decipher when following behind Parv in that torchlight. All of a sudden he came to a halt. The blue tiles were being invaded by long black boots that certainly did not belong to Parv. Without looking up, I squealed.

Getting caught (or may be not)

I began to tremble with fear as I knew this was the end. There was someone else present in the corridor which meant that our presence had been noticed and we had become exposed. We would now have to face the music for sure, regarding our presence at such an odd time inside the school building. My mind had started cooking up all kinds of stories already, though I dared not look up. The torch beamed on the floor, revealing two pairs of legs now. They belonged to Parv and that unknown black-booted presence. I awaited a showdown with my heart beating against my ribs.

"Meet Arora *sahib*...he is a good friend of mine." This was an unexpected way to begin a conversation. The moment I looked up with the torch beaming parallel to my nose, there stood a large frame of a body with a bare chest, holding something like a chisel in his hand. He did not look like any official, at least not with those rugged looks. He offered his hand to shake mine as I heaved a temporary sigh of relief. He made a growling noise.

“So do it…the stage is all yours Matka Bhai,” said Parv. Matka Bhai…a strange name! Matka Bhai again made a growling noise in response. I wondered whether he could speak even or not. His growls perfectly matched his animal-like body structure. I noticed his teeth looked more yellow than even the light of my torch. I directed the torch towards the door of the room in front of which we stopped and stood motionlessly: ‘EXAMINATION ROOM, in blue was embossed on the door.

“I have brought him along specially to make the keys for this lock. We actually don’t have to break the lock…quite a clean operation, you’ll see,” Parv said, grinning from ear to ear, with his white teeth shining bright. For the first time, I felt jealous of him. Matka Bhai was twisting and turning his chisel and doing something with the lock. I was trying to focus my eyes on the dark corridor with my torch focused on the lock. It took me some time to realise that something was crawling slowly on the top of my jeans and towards my crotch. Like a knee jerk reaction, I pushed away the hand and shrieked, “You son of a...”

Parv began to laugh loudly.

Seeing things in the darkness

Parv kept on holding the torch for me as I copied down the questions from the question paper that was dated two days ahead of time. It was actually quite foolish of me to note down the entire question paper with a pen on paper when it was printed in neat and small letters right there in front of me. The counter argument to this by Parv was that since the question papers came counted to the last page, if any were found missing, it would have spelt doom for everyone. We had found the question papers very neatly wrapped and sealed in a brown envelope when we reached the examination room. It was all due to Matka Bhai who we duly rewarded with one thousand rupees for his services. Parv immediately sent him off the campus and became preoccupied with a small steel ruler, a cutter and a brown sticking tape. He wanted to replace the seal that safeguarded the question papers. I was to note down the questions as I was considered to have a more legible handwriting than him (ahh…finally someone).

I had reached the eighth question out of the given 10 questions in no time. I wanted to finish it as fast as possible. The fear of getting caught reigned uppermost on my mind. As I was about to write down the given reaction, whose specific heat, was to be calculated, the whole room got engulfed in complete darkness.

"What the fuck?" I whispered, looking in the direction where Parv had stood a second before.

"I think the battery has given up…try doing it with the cell's display. I'll be right back," he replied with his voice going away from me, making me observe the Doppler's effect for the first time in my life (I was aware that I tended to get crazy thoughts at times).

"Where the fuck are you going?" I screamed, sure that there was no one around to hear us. The thought of being left alone was too scary a phenomenon for me.

"To find some solution for the dead batteries, *sahib*…I won't leave you alone. Darling, don't worry," he said as his voice trailed off into the distance. I now realised that I was all alone in that room. I pressed the 'unlock' button on my cell phone, increased the back light option from the settings and went back to the task of copying down the questions.

It took me around ten minutes to copy down the remaining two questions in the dim light. Parv hadn't returned yet. I put the question paper back into the envelope and sealed it cautiously with the brown sticking tape. It cost me some effort to get the stuff arranged again but I think I managed it pretty well in the end. I tried looking around the room with the mobile's display light to ensure that I hadn't left behind any telltale signs or any evidence of any human breaking into the room. Another ten minutes of careful inspection left me satisfied. I now looked around to search for any sign of Parv. I did not want to stay there any longer. Therefore, carrying the written piece of paper in my hand, I locked the room with the duplicate key and started walking back towards the stairs to depart. It was tough without any light to find my way out. I tried moving out purely on the basis of my intuition, hoping that Parv would turn up soon. As I was about to move down the stairs, I saw his dark figure standing beside the washroom. It was very hard to see in the dark but the shadow-like figure was enough to reveal that it was him. The figure wasn't moving but was standing still, rooted to a spot.

"Come down now, you asshole...I have got it. I would love to see the look on Chaturvedi's face when the results are declared. Come on now," I said, moving down the stairs and expecting him to follow. As I climbed down a few steps, I felt that there was no sound of steps following behind me. I waited for another few seconds, but still there was no noise! I turned to climb up the steps and stare at the washroom. No soul stood there. I rolled my eyes to focus better but found there was no one there. I looked left and then right, but there was no one around. Then, without thinking, I began to run as if a ghost followed behind to chase me. I ran so hard that I skipped some steps and jumped down. It was dark but it did not matter to me. The only thing that mattered was to make my escape from the building.

Chemistry – a piece of cake now but who was he?

"How come you came down so soon? And why did you run away from the washroom? What is wrong with you, *you ass?*" I heard as I was still trying to regain my breath on reaching the guardroom where Parv was sipping tea with the guards.

"I could not find the batteries and I thought you would do it *sahib*...! And for your information, I did not go anywhere near the washroom...I had cleaned my bowels already," he replied.

"You were not there?" I queried again.

"I swear I was not...in fact, I have been drinking tea with Ramesh Bhai since the past half hour. I came down the moment the torch went off...I hope you have locked up everything fine... chemistry is all set to be conquered now."

Hell!! He wasn't there...but how could it be? If it was not him, then who else was there? Maybe it was Matka Bhai, still trying to find his way out...but why would he take more than an hour to find a 100-metre way out? Wasn't it Parv? If he wasn't, then who was it? Would we be caught tomorrow? But if I wasn't able to see the person clearly, then he too could not have seen me either. My brain kept on analysing the situation which kept on getting more and more confusing with every new thought occurring in my mind. Parv dropped me home. It was 9:30 p.m. by my watch.

The next thing I did was to dial Noopur's number on my phone. She too had to appear for the supplementary exam.

"Hello...yeah Noopur? I know it's quite late in the night, but I was wondering if you too are appearing for the chemistry exam! Look...I have something to help all of us out...Parv and I went to the school...I know it was very dangerous...but you know *naah,* HOW MUCH I HATE CHEMISTRY..."

9

My Chemical Romance

"Thanks," she said, with her eyes lowered to the ground as she walked past me after the examination that day. She had ensured that when saying that six-lettered word, no one was around to hear her words. I was not even given a chance to reply for she zoomed past and I could not stop her mid-way. I knew I could reply to that 'thanks' later on in the evening on the phone. Leaking out the paper to her was going to earn me some favour in her eyes, I hoped. Though I still dreaded the thought of getting caught, I decided to go back to the classroom as all the other students were having their regular classes.

There were two things that were impossible to happen in my life this time, I thought:

- Humans finding the exact reason for the origin of universe
- Being around Parv and preventing him from touching me!

So here he was, coming from right behind me and putting his arm around my shoulders. I knew he felt those live vibes about us as we were supposed to be those long-lost friends and these vibes grew stronger as we had been partners in committing an evil deed. I was actually expecting him to say something regarding this, when he came and rolled his arm over mine, as we moved together towards the classroom.

"*Sahib,* any idea as to who could be behind those messages?"

"What? *Naah*…no…no, no, no. I don't have any idea," I said, caught off guard by his question. First, I hadn't expected it and second, I did have an idea but did not wish to reveal it. The build up to the supplementary examination had almost made me forget the dark incident that was gripping us all.

"But I heard something about Rahul from Aniket," he began, throwing a questioning look at me with his squinted eyes.

"Shut up…that's rubbish," I said. We had reached the classroom meanwhile and my pot of worries had started to overflow within me. I pushed his hand off my body and started looking around for Aniket. I definitely needed a talk. Before I could enter the classroom, I noticed the students forming a queue to come out. Over their heads my eyes fell on Mr. Chaturvedi who was guiding them from inside the classroom. They were going up the stairs to the laboratory for chemistry practical. As everyone emerged from the classroom, I noticed Aniket last in the queue and busy talking to a group that had broken apart from the well-organised queue. I slipped in silently into the queue, leaving Parv outside intentionally. Luckily for me, he joined another group of students.

I wanted to talk to Aniket urgently, but the presence of others around made me seal my lips and I decided to withhold everything till the lab session got over. We had to perform the practical experiments in groups of twos and threes and very deliberately

I joined the group that included Noopur. I pulled Aniket along with me too as I needed to talk to him about his sudden rude behaviour towards Rahul. The lab assistant was still busy setting up the instruments required, thus providing the much needed opportunity to talk.

"What's wrong with you?" I finally asked Aniket in a severe tone when both of us stood apart from our group.

"What? Nothing."

"Nothing? You said something to me regarding Rahul that night and I heard the same thing from Parv today. Don't you think you are going a bit too far in your assessment of Rahul?" I asked, wearing a dejected look on my face. I glanced sideways and around to see if anyone was watching us or not and found Parv looking suspiciously at us from the far right corner of the lab. He queried through the movement of his eyes as to what was afoot. I quickly moved my eyes away and noticed Noopur standing there. I looked towards Parv again and made my lips move silently as if asking, *'What?'* He too looked in the same direction and pointed with a nod in the other direction. I steered my eyes away and noticed Saumil standing right next to Noopur. He was telling her something while she was smiling back. My heart beats began to jump as I wondered, *'What was that?'*

"*Bol naah*...why are you dumb now?" I asked, chaffing at the scene recently witnessed and looking towards Aniket.

"Arori...*marna hai?* I told you everything. I don't understand where your mind wanders off these days!" he replied. I heard him though my attention was on Noopur standing and talking with Saumil as if she had known him since long. Oh...first things first! Here I need to draw up a verbal sketch of this person to justify the reason for fretting (because I don't think I would like to mention him anywhere again).

Saumil Saxena, lovingly known as Saumi, was a so-called stud of the school. I am told girls drooled over him when he first joined school. He was not so fair of complexion, had a lean structure, wore a stupid goatee to support his weird facial expressions, walked with his legs apart like a chimpanzee and had unkempt and not so great-looking spiky hair. In short, he looked more like an ape to me. He was known to be adept in weaving tales and telling whoever cared to listen that he was interested in developing animations and had been receiving calls from the top universities of the world. One month he would say that he was going to the USA after Class XII exam and the next month his base would shift to Australia or Canada and what not. It always seemed that he was constantly going on a world tour and as expected, people like me could never believe his words (and rightly so). But as is the case with girls, they used to fall prey to his tall stories and lap up all that he said. In any case, there was no doubt about his story-making abilities. Was it any wonder that within the first three or four months of his school stay, he had a range of girlfriends, ranging from the junior to the secondary level, drooling over him. Now the question was why should it have bothered me? Well, girls being very gullible are always easy to trap but at the same time are equally adept in realising a person's potential. So it was discovered that it took no time for his girlfriends to soon become his ex because once his real talent was discovered, they discarded him like burning coals. By now his stature in the school had fallen considerably. So here he was all alone, close to Noopur and talking to her. Fuck, why was she smiling at him! Parv too was giggling in one corner.

The apparatus had been set up and so Aniket and I moved closer to where Noopur and Saumil stood. He was trying to show his genius by fiddling with the apparatus. Mr. Chaturvedi stood up from the teacher's table and drew closer to all of us. He came and stood in the centre in order to explain the procedure of the experiment. I was still casting sideward glances to find out what Saumil was up to. After completing his instructions, Mr. Chaturvedi asked all of us to proceed ahead with the experiment to be performed.

Comparison of the rate of evaporation of different liquids was the aim of our experiment. With my head bent, I began to concentrate on performing the practical. For a person like me who had no interest in the subject, it was crushingly dull to learn about tiny things that couldn't even be seen and write out inferences as to what happened to them. I heated up the different liquids provided to us all and cooled them down. Then I mixed them all together and waited to see the result. Mr. Chaturvedi continued to explain the minor details of the experiment though by reading from our lab manual – "When a liquid is placed in an open vessel, it slowly escapes in the form of gas, eventually leaving the vessel empty. This phenomenon is known as evaporation."

I straightened up and looked towards Saumil and Noopur, before bending down to my experiment. I tried to recall the words again that Mr. Chaturvedi had spoken and felt that I too was like an open vessel with Saumil being the gas and Noopur, the liquid within the vessel. The vessel was getting empty and my heart was evaporating. I pinched myself, trying to remind myself not to react to the chemistry taking place between the two of them.

Mr. Chaturvedi continued, "Evaporation of liquids can be explained on the basis of the kinetic molecular model. Though there are strong inter-molecular attractive forces which hold the molecules of a liquid together, the molecules have sufficient kinetic energy to escape in the gaseous form if the molecules happen to come near the surface."

He spoke about the strong inter-molecular attraction that held the molecules together. I began to have doubts about my strong interpersonal attraction with Noopur but the law said that the molecules possessing sufficient energy tended to escape into the gas phase. Was Saumil the required kinetic energy? Was my intermolecular force not sufficiently strong?

Mr. Chaturvedi continued, "In any liquid, all the molecules do not possess the same kinetic energy. A small fraction of molecules which have enough kinetic energy to overcome the force of attraction escape into the gas phase."

Ahh…finally something positive, I thought. According to this, the girls around me had different affinity towards the gaseous phase *(read as Saumil).* Only a small fraction of molecules *(read as girls)* could escape the vessel *(read as me).* This implied that the probability of the escape of my required molecules (*that is, Noopur*) was less. I thanked chemistry for that.

Mr. Chaturvedi said, "If the liquid is taken in an open vessel, evaporation continues till the whole of the liquid evaporates."

That was the final nail in my coffin. If all the liquid was to evaporate, then what would be left would be the open vessel. No strong forces mattered then. My brain rang an alarm bell and out of nowhere appeared the question: "Sir, what if the vessel was kept covered?"

The whole class turned to look at me with amazement.

"Mr. Aurore, the liquid will then keep on coming back towards the vessel only," replied Mr. Chaturvedi, no less surprised than the rest of the class.

"Yes!" I hissed. Everybody glanced at me and looked away to concentrate on their experiment. Mr. Chaturvedi had failed to notice my exclamation.

"Arori…I'll take you to my Dad today. You need a check-up," Aniket said. I did not reply. I had to cover the vessel and prevent my liquid from escaping. I heard Saumil explain to Noopur the procedure for the experiment, which involved the use of three chemicals. These had to be sucked through a pipette (a glass tube) and then placed in a petri dish, to allow it to evaporate. The time taken to complete the evaporation had to be jotted down. I overheard him mention acetone, one of the chemicals to be used. It is also used in nail-polish removers and if consumed, it could lead to shivers in the body. My brain had chalked out a plan already. The vessel had to be covered and as I was in the same group as Noopur, I was to help them out.

Aniket was busy gossiping with Parv. So I went ahead and offered to help out Saumil. Noopur glanced at me once but soon looked away, blowing in through the pipette. I could never describe the expression that came to her face then. Anyway it was decided that Saumil would suck the liquids through the pipette and I would tell him when to stop sucking so that the liquid would not enter his mouth. The first liquid to be sucked in through the pipette was benzene. He sucked it in and I told him to stop. He did as told and all went well. He even cracked a silly joke while taking in chloroform through the pipette. Noopur looked at me and just smiled *(still cannot explain what it meant).* I stopped him again at the right time to prevent him from inhaling the chloroform. "That's easy," he said. Now it was the turn to take acetone.

"It's so easy...one single suck and we are done," he said, looking proudly towards Noopur.

So he sucked the acetone but I did not stop him. The next thing was to see him rush to the washroom with his mouth open and dripping acetone on the floor and the class laughing from behind.

"Sir, such a stupid fellow he is! He said he was thirsty," I said in my bid to place the final lid on the covered vessel. The whole class again burst into laughter, while Mr. Chaturvedi rushed to the washroom to follow him.

"What a stupid person he is," I said, looking towards Noopur. She did not say anything except to give a small smile (*maybe in support of my action*)...

Later in the day, when the final bell rang, I noticed Saumil ask Noopur hand him his bike helmet which he had kept behind her desk. He said something to her and she replied smilingly. My heart beats rose again as I left the classroom, looking completely dismayed. This hole in the covered vessel had to be filled up soon...

* * * * *

It has been said that there is a very close relationship between love and jealousy where "jealousy knows no bounds while love binds people."

I was in an agitated state of mind and the world too seemed to be in an unfamiliar state to me. I did not eat my so favourite Punjabi *kadhi* that day on returning from school. Eating would not have made a difference to my senses which had become numb. My eyes could see the same picture over and over again: Saumil speaking, Noopur smiling. It was like a low-quality pirated DVD that gets stuck on the same devillish sequence and all I could do was to close my eyes in frustration. Actually it did not concern the eyes alone; even the brain kept coming back to the same thoughts again and again. Nothing else seemed to exist around me except for the realisation that she was going far from my reach all of a sudden, at short notice. I remembered Manu getting restless and upset when Carol was going away to Mumbai. There hadn't been a single moment that day when I could not feel the pain that Manu had done. Maybe there was something in the analogy that I was facing when I too needed to take drastic action as Manu had done.

The coaching class on that evening wasn't anything unusual as we studied the 'wave motion' theory in physics, 'probability' in mathematics and ironically, 'vapour liquid equilibrium' in chemistry (which I very deliberately avoided listening). But there was an uneasiness that was gripping me at a constantly increasing rate. I had lost all interest in talking to anyone around me; not even to Aniket. My teeth gritted against each other and I wasn't sure whether it marked anger or helplessness at my situation. This was doing no good to me and I was so agitated that I desperately needed to find a solution to my condition.

Aniket stopped midway when we were on our way back home. He had received a call from Neha and he asked me whether I wanted to be dropped home first. Very gallantly I refused. I did not want to go back and lie down on my bed and remember the things that had been hurting me. He very happily picked up the phone and went far away from me, to indulge in some private talk. I sat back on the ever-hurting pillion of his scooter and watched the traffic passing by. It took me a few seconds to revert to my thought process despite trying to look at the advertisement hoardings. I just could not divert my attention. There was this big Adidas advertisement that stood in the far corner of the road. A crippled boy was shown playing soccer and the tagline read, 'Impossible is nothing!' On the other corner of the road was an Airtel cell-phone advertisement that said, 'Barriers break when we talk!' It really was amazing to find how small things could be so riveting as to almost decide our whole lives on their basis. Sometimes even the slightest hope can bring back the dead. The solution to my problem lay right in front of me: I had to perform the impossible – break the barrier and talk! I looked back at Aniket who was still talking and smiling. A few yards away from him stood a shop, claiming to provide quick Airtel recharges. I moved towards it when Aniket yelled, "What Arori? Want to make a phone call? To whom?"

"It's high time we covered the vessel, mate," I screamed back. He gave a thumb up in return. I quickly got my phone reloaded and chose a secluded corner to make my phone call. I did not want anyone to hear my conversation nor did I want to listen to the noise the vehicular traffic made when passing by. This was going to be the most important phone call of my life.

I dialled her number and waited for exactly thirty-two seconds before she picked up, though those thirty-two seconds were enough to make my cardiogram reveal the world's highest peaks. Nevertheless I was amazed at the confidence with which I was operating. It hadn't taken me much time to decide what I had to do.

"Hi!" she said.

"Hey!" I replied.

"You called up at the right time. I have just returned back from a *pooja*." I felt the usual depth of divinity and solace that I found when talking to her. She seemed to be panting which probably was due to the short distance she must have had to cover to receive my call. For a change, I felt in complete command over myself.

"How is your mood, today?" I asked point blank.

She immediately shot back, "Why? Is there something special today?"

"I need to know about your mood. How is it?" I repeated agitatedly.

"It is fine. But why so suddenly such a…."

I just heard till 'it is fine' because by this time my mind had started working on how I was going to say what I had been wanting, since seeing her smile at Saumil. "Noopur, I am not sure whether it's the right time to say this but I think it has been long enough for me to realise what I feel within my heart. I still remember the day I first saw you – a cute little girl with snowy skin…that time I never imagined I would get to know you ever, but then we talked, heard each other's life story and tried to study each other better. At least that is what I did. I have no hesitation in stating that you are the most beautiful girl that I have ever met in my life and after knowing you better, I have found you to be still more beautiful. I believe what I feel for you is above anything else and I have ever felt for anyone else. I have been spending sleepless nights thinking about you and even in sleep, I have been dreaming about you. I have had to reveal all this to you because I cannot keep it bottled up within me much longer. It has taken me some time to admit this but Noopur, I think I like you more than a friend!"

Dead silence followed! Pure dead silence! My pulse began to race at a high speed, though I managed to maintain my composure as my lips did the talking. But she did not react. I could hear the background voices because there was pin-drop silence while she pondered what to reply. I waited for a few seconds for her reply but she stood dead still as a rock.

"Say something *ab*... at least," I requested.

"What? Give me some time to get over the shock first," she replied. Her reply aroused some hope in my chest and waited eagerly for her reply.

"But I am waiting...alright…no…take your time…I am holding on."

"Waiting as in? I am not telling you anything right now! I need to think…" she said stubbornly but not harshly or rudely.

"Not now? But I thought you would give an answer right now and I would be able to clear my head…how much time do you need, huh?"

"Maybe till tomorrow…I won't take much more," she responded.

"But we don't get to talk in school. How will you tell me then? And by the way, is there any chance of your reply being positive?" I asked, amazed at my own audacity. I was surprised at the firmness I was displaying.

"Call me up in the evening then, *naah*…and stay hopeful. I haven't given an answer yet."

This is what I would have exactly called as poisoning slowly. I knew it was going to be a long anxious night followed by a long scary day. But I was willing to wait and in any case what other option did I have? I had put the ball in her court; now it was her turn to lob it in my court.

We continued to talk as if nothing had happened between us. I visualised calm and serene face which had a soothing effect on me. I went on to tell her how I turned still every time I saw her, how I turned poetic in my thoughts about her, who all were the girls I had a crush on till date, how Saumil had acted as a catalyst in making me reveal my feelings to her and what not. She also gave me an account of her life, what all she thought about me and what an idiot Saumil was *(Wow! I just wanted to jump with joy!).* I wanted our conversation to continue endlessly but there was no balance left in my SIM card and I had to hang up abruptly. Though greatly disappointed, I heaved a sigh of relief at having done what I wanted to do. There was no more any pain in my heart. I began to walk towards the scooter, satisfaction writ large on my face. On hearing the ring call on my cell phone, I halted midway and looked at the caller's number. It was Noopur.

"Yeah?" I began excitedly.

"I was wondering if you would like to have my reply just now itself!"

"Right now? But didn't you say it was to be tomorrow?" I asked foolishly.

"If you want it tomorrow…then it's okay by me. You don't want it right now, then it is alright by me."

"No...no…I want your reply desperately. I cannot wait till tomorrow. If you were to tell it right now, you cannot imagine how relieved I would be and be able to sleep peacefully tonight," I said, sounding desperate but positive.

"You sure you want to hear it right now?" she asked again.

"Absolutely."

"Yes?"

"What?" I exclaimed in confusion.

"YES …it's a yes, stupid."

I wanted to jump up and touch the sky with happiness but how could I behave so childishly? A deathly silence followed though I could hear her breathing hard. I wanted to go in the middle of the road and perform a jig; I wanted to remove those advertisements on the hoardings and tell the world what I was feeling. A large smile played on my lips, making it impossible to utter a single word. Sometimes silence can be more meaningful than words.

"You are shocked I suppose. I need to put down the phone though, because if Mom were to catch me, this happy beginning will surely come to an abrupt end," she said, breaking the silence.

"I am short of words, I swear. I want to say so many things but they are just not coming out."

"I know…it's okay. We will talk tomorrow and then you can tell me the rest of the things you want me to hear. Dear, goodnight."

"Yeah…goodnight," I said, my head floating in the clouds.

"Sweet dreams," she added.

"Sweet dreams," I responded.

"Anything else that you want to say?" she asked.

"No…I think it's enough for today," I said laughingly.

"Okay…'bye," she said sweetly and put down the phone. I moved back to the scooter where Aniket sat, waiting for me. He gave me a fist to fist after hearing the word-by-word narration I gave him. Then we drove back home, though I kept on wondering if I had missed to say something which she expected me to say, something after 'sweet dreams'?

10

Things get Murkier

It was no problem for me to get away from home as it was easy to deal with Mom any day than Dad. Neha was coming to Jaipur and so Aniket had decided to throw a small party for all of us. I was eager to tell Mom where all we were going that Sunday afternoon with Neha, who was Aniket's long-time girlfriend. She could be pretty cool with such things and I too could confide all my secrets to her (though I wanted to keep the fact of having a girlfriend away from her as long as possible.) I had such a good rapport with Mom that my friends used to tease me that I was Mama's boy still. As for Dad, he trusted me completely and none of my not-so-good acts ever came to light in front of him.

I took a light breakfast and reached Aniket's home thirty minutes before the scheduled time. I waited for fifteen seconds before he emerged from the room, looking his best and with his hands curling around his hair. No wonder, the presence of a princess had turned the frog into a prince.

"*Chal*...I've got to buy some stuff."

"Stuff? You won't get the opportunity in the crowd there," I said, dissuading him from taking such a step.

"Doggy…not that stuff. I want to buy something for Neha. *Chal.*"

"Ohhh…" I mumbled under my breath.

After another 200 metres of riding, I stopped my bike right in front of the nearest gift shop. Aniket got off from the bike and rushed into the gift shop as I put my bike on the side stand. I too went inside the shop. The air-conditioned shop was any day better than the scorching heat outside. He kept on scouting the shop from left to right, probably looking for something unusual while the shopkeeper kept on gazing at our activity. Suddenly we came to a halt because Aniket had found a couple of gift cards along with soft toys. I too looked around, hoping to find something eye-catching. I asked Aniket for his opinion and his toll of soft toys increased to three with the cute thing that I had bought. "Asshole," I mouthed. Exactly twenty minutes later, with Aniket poorer by 530 bucks, we reached his home with all the 'stuff' kept inside a polybag that was hung on one side of the bike. His Mom and Dad stood right there at the entrance of their home, looking quite angry through their red blazing eyes.

"Sonuuuu…now you are not going anywhere. Come inside right now," his Dad screamed.

"Why? What has happened?" he squawked.

"That I'll tell you once you come inside…it's Rahul's birthday, I know…you have been lying to us thinking that we wouldn't know of it. Come back right now," it was his Mom's turn to scream now in a voice louder than any that I had heard so far.

"I am not coming…you don't know a damn thing and yet you are going on talking nonsense…let's go Aadi."

'Why me?'

"We don't know...we don't know. We don't know who Neha is? Other people are messaging me on my mobile to say that my son is up to something and don't think that I will let you get away easily..." So saying, his Dad held him from his wrist and dragged him inside. His Mom followed behind while I stood back against my bike, as if in a state of shock. I did not know how to react to this – whether to go away or wait for Aniket whose 'stuff' still hung around my bike. One thing was certain though and it was that Aniket's Dad had received some SMS from somewhere and he was frightened and worried for his son's well-being. It really meant that the problem had snowballed into something which must have made Aniket see red. Rahul's face came in front of my eyes and my brain started to work overtime. I could hear loud voices coming from Aniket's house. I felt quite awkward standing there, thinking that he would come out. *I was being insane,* I kept on telling myself and cursing the person who had caused the trouble. I feared that possibly Aniket was being thrashed by his parents. Someone was playing a dirty game and making things tough for Aniket, who was as helpless as a fly in a spider's web. I was still confused as to what I could do next when the door of his house was flung open with a loud bang.

"Let's go, Aadi," he said, a grim scowl plastered on his face. From the corner of my eyes I noticed his Mom and Dad follow behind him.

"Stop Sonuuuu...," his Mom called but he didn't care to listen to her.

"What happened? What next?" I asked as he sat down on my bike's pillion.

"Run..."

"What?" I exclaimed with shock.

"I said...run."

The moment he uttered the word again, I started my bike and raced it as if competing with the wind. My eyes did look once at his Dad who was saying something, probably to me, but in the noise of the bike engine, I could not hear anything. I knew explanations of any kind would not have made any difference to them.

"What the hell happened?" I asked him the moment we were about a hundred metres away from his home.

"Don't ask me…I am going to kill that guy today for sure. How the fuck could he send a message to my Dad's cell…how the fuck! Just because I had kept quiet did not mean that I had forgotten what he had done. I will not allow him to do whatever he wants. I even told you that he was the one who has been involved in all this and look, even Dad is following behind to check where we are headed," he replied while dialling Neha's number.

I was in such a situation that first of all I had to find a way to calm down Aniket and second, I had to think of a way to dodge Aniket's Dad. There was a third problem though and it was that there seemed to be no way out of our predicament. The moment Aniket kept down his phone, I started playing my part of trying to calm him down, telling him that we still did not have any proof of Rahul's involvement in the game that was being played on us. We had no solid proof to back Aniket's claim or of accusing Rahul *(damn, I was tired of doing this again and again).* And as always, good sense prevailed just before we reached our destination.

I saw everyone waiting with anticipation and crowded around the lone female figure of Neha. The very moment I saw her, I thought, 'Aniket has a cherry in his mouth.' She looked frightened to the core and rightly so, considering the situation. I exchanged an 'hi' with everyone, who all stood quite subdued.

Aniket and Neha stood beside each other, though I don't think that any words were exchanged between them. It was merely their eyes that were doing the talking I suppose. The world surrounding love can be starkly different.

"Aniket...what has happened?" Rahul asked, coming forward towards us. I counted the number of people who were present. We were six in all – Rahul, Aniket, Neha, Manu, Parv (why was he here?) and I. There was no reply from Aniket. Sensing the gravity of the situation, I went and stood in the centre of this small group to explain the whole scenario to everyone. Rahul threw a filthy expression at Aniket but the latter ignored it.

"So...it means...the day has been screwed," Manu began as I drew to the end of my narrative. I looked towards Parv, expecting him to say something but he remained quiet, strangely enough.

"Who is doing this *yaar*... this is spoiling all the fun. Why is it taking you so long to catch the culprit, Aniket?" Rahul said, looking towards Aniket for a reply. The latter gave no reply but looked with obvious disgust at the speaker. Neha still stood quietly beside him, convincing me that not a single word had been exchanged by them.

"Leave it for the moment. His Dad will be here any moment and we can't afford to be seen with Neha among us," I said with a look of concern on my face. Though not very well enacted, I was able to portray my emotions quite correctly.

"We can switch over places; Café Piano is just about three kilometres away from here...what do you say?" Manu asked. That was a good idea actually but contained a few loopholes. We were standing in front of the restaurant called 'Little India' which was the venue for Rahul's birthday celebrations as told to Aniket's parents. Switching over places was fine but if his Dad was to come and find us missing from there, it would have provided him enough reason to believe that the allegations made by the SMS were correct. Even if Aniket was to tell them the new location, there was every likelihood of his Dad reaching there to check personally. In short, we were caught between assumptions and realities. Time was running out and we hadn't reached a solution yet.

"How about splitting up? Aniket takes Neha off from here while two of us can stay behind to check whether his Dad is coming or not. If he comes, he will find the two to help him face the situation easily. Once we are sure about the situation, we can regroup. We will lose some time but still it would be worth it," said Manu. I realised he was getting wiser day by day since the time he had met Carol. So we had quite a full-proof plan ready with us. Obviously Aniket was going to take away Neha on a route that was different than his Dad would take, so that it would not be possible for his Dad to come searching. That amounted to taking a longer route to avoid running into his Dad. It meant getting time to spend with a gorgeous girl, I thought. The two of us were to stay behind where we were and I was happy with this arrangement as I would any day prefer to be with Rahul than with the saliva-dripping Parv. (*It would have been not easy to avoid rape with him around*). Besides, both of us were the most sensible amongst the lot (*a general perception*) and more adept at handling irksome situations. Manu and Parv were to reach the restaurant we had identified and be the first ones to enjoy the food before any of us could. We were planning action to face the sender of silly messages without knowing who the sender was. Fear can be so devastating!

"This is insane…seriously…we have to do something to sort this out. This can't continue for long," said Rahul to me as we both rested our bums on his bike's pillion after everyone had left. Aniket had taken away my bike.

"Yeah…it has reached the limit now. Earlier I used to shrug it off just as a prank but this is getting really serious. I never thought someone could actually do this," I replied, trying to be objective in my views. I was convinced that he was not the one for whom we were looking.

"Yeah…just need to get one hint and we will catch that son of a bitch by his neck," he added. I remained quiet. I did not want to reveal that Aniket already had some vague suspicions which did not augur well for him. I was the one who was on tenterhooks. I glanced at the far end of the road to check if anything suspicious was to be seen. All I could see was the receding back of Aniket on his bike, slowly weaving his way through the dense traffic. Parv had zoomed off the scene at a fast speed.

"Is his Dad coming or not?" Rahul sighed.

"No idea at all…keep looking at the other end though…he may be arriving any time…be ready."

"We don't have to look at both the ends; the other end is surely safe. Who will possibly take a ten-kilometre route to reach a place which is just two kilometres away? Forget the far end...if it was I, I would never have come from the far end. By the way, if his Dad thinks out of the box and decides to come from the other end, Aniket will be screwed; he will be caught red handed with Neha…Ha! Ha!" laughed Rahul, winking at me. I did not find it funny at all. My funny bone had gone for a walk since the scene I had witnessed in the morning.

"Whatever. Be on the lookout wherever you can," I replied. Nearly fifteen minutes elapsed but there was no sign of anybody. We were informed that Manu and Parv had reached Café Piano. We both kept on chatting about the usual stuff. The sun had risen high in the sky and I could feel the heat on my skin. I looked at the most probable end of the road from which he could come but noticed the usual traffic hovering. Just for a brief second, I looked at the other side and took my eyes away. I looked back again and felt I had noticed something for sure. There was some movement off the road. I put on my spectacles and carefully looked at the far end. A green Zen car was coming at crawling pace through the traffic at the far end. I looked more carefully and I found Aniket's Dad driving the car and his little brother looking around on both sides of the road. I turned to look at Rahul, whose eyes were staring at me. Just for a second our eyes locked and the next moment both of us screamed together…

"Run."

* * * * *

The moment the green Zen moved away from the restaurant, both of us emerged from behind the restaurant building, where we had hidden ourselves. Aniket's Dad had halted the car for about five minutes after checking every nook and corner around. For all those five minutes my heart stood still as if it had forgotten to beat.

"Why the fuck did you run?" I scowled at Rahul as soon as he started the bike.

"Me? You only screamed out to tell me to run," he replied as he moved the bike out of the parking lot.

"What? It was you," I protested. We both knew that our mind had left us the moment we had seen the green Zen draw near. Despite being aware of the fact that we had to stay there and make sure that Aniket's Dad did not go unsatisfied, we knew we had screwed the situation. The very thought of confronting his Dad had frightened the daylights out of us both. I was still hoping that his Dad would have noticed Rahul's bike parked outside the restaurant and been relieved at finding the truth in the story surrounding Rahul's birthday.

It took us another ten minutes to reach Café Piano where we both began to fling abuses at each other. None of us was willing to accept his fault. We entered the restaurant and saw everyone sitting comfortably around the tables, looking perfectly relaxed. It seemed as if nothing had ever happened. We both too joined in. I had a few words to add though, before I sat down.

"Aniket, don't know what it is going to be like when you reach home...but for the moment, as far as we are together and you are alive (I winked), let's make the best of the time together in the hope that your Dad doesn't reach here and no more messages screw our day."

We all raised our fists and struck them in the air. Parv intentionally touched my fist (c'mon, his touch couldn't be unintentional). Another five minutes passed before my cell beeped and a message appeared on the screen: *'Isn't it a wondrful thot if I tell his dad d new locatn...party spoilt? lol...dun wry...ill let u enjy dis tym!P*

I looked at all their faces which were busy smiling and talking to each other. I pressed the delete button, pushed the cell inside my pocket and started smiling...

11

The Naked Chick

Location: *Room number 205, Parv's hostel.*
Time: *18:30 hours.*
Day: *The same screwed day of Aniket's life.*
Reason for this write up: *He screwed it back!*
How do I know: *We all saw it, didn't we?*

"Okay, alright! Are we actually doing this?" Manu asked, raising an eyebrow as I pushed open the window of Room Number 105 on the first floor.

"You don't believe me, right?" I asked, forcing my head out to check the distance between the second floor window and our window.

"Mr. Pandey! Our eyes are up for a feast today. Stop bothering your ass and just enjoy," Rahul said as he followed me on to the shaft outside the window. Manu waited for a minute, pondered and then followed in our footsteps.

Yeah...I need to explain this. It was the evening of the same eventful Sunday when we had gone to celebrate Rahul's fake birthday (*and you thought it was over with that SMS? Well...I thought the same too*). I had satisfied all my cravings for food that day, thanks to the free lunch sponsored by Aniket. Friends' girlfriends aren't that bad a thing to have! I thought the day had ended well until Aniket's desires started acquiring a new shape (*don't ask me about the geometrical aspect of the shape*). A hasty plan was drawn up to show Neha the hostel where Parv stayed. Okay, I admit, my head had not started working at that point of time but well, it eventually did work at some point at least. It was a Sunday and most of the guys had either gone back home or were out of the hostel, passing time in the city malls. None of us had a problem in joining the couple for a visit. There wasn't any harm in it after all. It was just a visit to the hostel, though Aniket suggested a couple of times that we should be heading back home as he had to drop Neha home for which none of us were required anyway. There are times when we tend to leave all the morals and ethics back in the cupboard and invite trouble. I was definitely in the Satanic frame of mind when I realised that something crooked was going on in Aniket's mind. I wanted to linger around and find out what was on his mind.

The hostel was deserted and whatever of the crowd was left was taken away by Parv. He, as always, was bent on showing his dedication to Aniket, his absence though was greatly appreciated by me. Now what Aniket wanted was to get rid of us. I made the task easier for him by directing Manu and Rahul to occupy Room Number 204 which was Ayush's room. Obviously, the action was to begin once we were out of sight. Aniket, as expected, moved quietly into Room Number 205 which was Parv's room. Neha wanted us all to be present but we refused and started playing on the PC placed in the room. I, at seventeen had access to sexual visuals available only on the internet or the 'animal planet' and I was definitely not into the animal thing. I was sure of Aniket's fascination for the hostel because that is where such things could happen. He was a guy and she was a girl; they were madly in love and all by themselves in that room. Do I need to explain any more about the setup?

I may have given it all up if Rahul hadn't shown the same inclination towards the Satanic thought arising in my mind. Manu was frightened, making me wonder if his otherwise bold exterior had gone for a walk that day. The room was bolted in another fifteen minutes and we were ready to witness the scenes inside Room Number 205 from the room where we were in at that moment. As the windows did not have any shaft in between, we could not move to the other window to grasp the scene (if there was any!). The only option was to move to the floor below the room and try climbing up on the shafts in between the first and the second floor. Since there wasn't anyone in the hostel, reaching the first shaft in between wasn't difficult. They both just had to give a little lift to their lighter bodies while I had to struggle a bit to push myself up the climb.

"You want me to break my leg before you or am I getting a demo first?" Manu asked and he moved back as he looked towards the second shaft that was our destination to a heavenly view. It was tricky for all three of us to balance on a single shaft and as he moved, we had to make sure no one among us tipped over. A bone or two was sure to crack, otherwise. The second shaft was a bit far away than what I had calculated down at the window.

"I am getting out of this because I know it isn't going to work!" Manu said, jumping down from the first shaft back on to the window. I pondered over the available options.

"Pass me that helmet in the room before you go away," I said, showing no intention of stopping him. He gave me a surprised look before handing me the helmet without any change in expression. The advantage of the helmet was that it gave us an extra few inches of height.

"Will it work?" Rahul asked as I placed the helmet on the narrow space we were standing on.

"I don't know," I said. The second shaft was still further above. Only a perfect jump could have led me to the destination. I also had to ensure that not even a bit of noise was made if we wanted our plan to succeed. It really was scary, but the reward we expected was going to make up for it. I realised much later in life that every guy has two different hemispheres in his brain – one which is logical and the other which is irrational and leads to trouble, thrives on sex and is responsible for making a man out of a boy!

It was the second part of my brain that was in a superior position, making me hopeful of seeing some fascinating things. It was, however, irrational because I was in a hurry to be a man soon. I put my first foot on the helmet and pressed the second foot against the shaft to give my body the required thrust. A couple of false starts followed by a perfect push made me airborne. It was so Pokemon like. Yeah…I had seen that in my tender years. While I jumped, the world around dissolved and revolved in a magical way! I knew if it was to be captured on a camera, the visuals would have looked mindblowing in slow motion. As I landed on the second shaft, I looked back towards Manu, wagging my tongue at him. He mouthed a couple of abuses but I did not care. A couple of minutes later, Rahul too joined me on the shaft, thereby depriving me of the thrill of being the only one to perform the stunt that I had. For another minute or so, we looked towards each other while staying crouched under the window and I noticed that mischievous look in Rahul's eyes which told us a it was that precious moment.

That was it! It was a naked female body, nude to the core. Aniket was there too but I hardly noticed whether he was half naked or full. I had seen myself naked all my life and Aniket would have looked only worse, not better. My eyes focused on the main point and all the other points were just blurred reflections. Aniket and the room came in the blurred part while my eyes were focused on the gorgeous parts of the naked female. Yes, sex it was! My first time ever I was witnessing real-life visuals! No videos or blue rays could have matched the clarity and the detailed depth that my eyes offered. I could feel the smoothness of that exposed skin from the distance even. The curves swayed as the body moved like a snake under the charmer's effect. She was fleshy but the flesh was at perfect places and I loved looking at it. Dark brown stiffened nipples on the tempting round breasts provided the perfect background for seduction. With every touch, they fluffed with that bouncing effect that immediately led me to think of the 'Johnson's baby soap' advertisement which showed a baby's butt being pulled and then vibrating. Aniket's lips sucked the freshness of the skin as they lay down on the bed. Every little thing that was being done by him to her, increased my heart beats with every passing moment. Each movement exposed more of her and I could only marvel at a naked female body which must have been God's most beautiful creation! Blood flowed through my veins to activate those testosterones and I could feel the twitch in my bottoms. I looked towards Rahul, who was so engrossed in the scene that he least cared about the bulge near his abdomen. I was getting pushed at times so that he could get that little extra glimpse or that little better angle to the action. Aniket kept stroking her as we kept on staring with our mouths wide open and tongues wagging. I could listen to the sounds of pleasure in the pain she was supposedly having. She clung on to him, with every little curve of hers perfectly resting on to his muscles. He carried her up from the bed with his entire strength and pushed her against the wall. We had to duck once to escape detection but since they were too engrossed in the act, we popped up again. She had the same delirious expression on her face that I had witnessed in every damn porno I had watched so far. She was beautiful without her clothes and her butt was cuter than those kids in the 'baby soap' ads, and fluffier!

An older boy had advised me that disturbing a couple involved in the sexual act was the biggest moral crime in God's rule book and it became more severe when done to animals. I was sure I wasn't performing a crime out there. First, they weren't animals and second, was I disturbing them? In fact I was just admiring God's reasons for introducing sex in our lives. I wasn't yet an adult but sex occupied my mind. I was learning – learning through them that it wasn't a crime, was it?

"What?" I heard Manu's hoarse voice say and I pulled myself away with a jerk. As a result, my body moved all of a sudden and with a resounding thud, Manu landed on the first shaft. I had committed the crime. I had disturbed the sexes in the sex!

"Run," I said hoarsely to Rahul.

"Again?"

"Jump!" I said as jumping was a better action and he understood that well. I took his hand and made him jump back on to the first shaft where Manu was shrieking with pain. I supported a limping Manu to the exit. The next target was Room Number 204. With the kind of commotion we had created, I anticipated that the love act would have come to an abrupt end and it really did as Aniket threw open the door of Room Number 204 to find us seated on the PC. We had been quick to return to the room despite the fact that Manu had been badly hurt. He was, however, trying to put up a brave act, though I feared that he may have broken a bone or two.

"It was boring without you people. You should have been in our room," Aniket said as Neha appeared from behind. She looked tired. The obvious reason we knew.

Rahul and I exchanged knowing glances with each other. To me the girl seemed to be without clothes as I had noticed her not very long ago. I certainly wouldn't have minded joining in, right?

"It's okay. Next time we all will be right there with you!" Rahul smirked. I laughed quietly.

We all headed out of the hostel, with Aniket and Neha leading the way. I was supporting Manu, who was still finding it tough to balance himself on both his feet.

"Was that good?" he asked me, trying to suppress his voice as we moved out.

"Oh yeah, completely! You missed all the education you could have got…your birthright."

Gaining knowledge isn't a crime and disturbing someone while you gain it isn't that bad either – Lord Almighty, I hope you are listening!

12

My First Date

I had to squeeze this one in between, despite taking into account what all was happening around. Aniket was in a mess for sure and Neha had gone back to her place (she still occurred naked in my dreams). The messages had come to a halt, though it was only forty-eight hours since the last one came. Strangely enough and to our surprise, Aniket wasn't pulled up at his home. The only outcome after his amorous adventure was that his whereabouts were being kept under vigil and his each move scrutinised. What about me? Well, I was kind of enjoying life. The 'dreaded SMS-man', the one who had been sending threatening messages, despite knowing my phone number, no longer seemed in a mood to bother me and that was pretty cool for me. Maybe his accounts with me were all in good faith, but deep inside, I still longed to know who that son of a bitch was. Nobody was happy with the happenings all around.

Ohh...yeah…to come back to the point, it was two days after that particular Sunday afternoon, that is, Tuesday to be precise

(Mahatma Gandhi's birthday and a public holiday), when it wasn't noon exactly, some minutes less than it (which remained the trademark time forever), Noopur and her friend Vartika visited the Fun Kingdom Amusement Park, some six kilometres away from my home and sixteen kilometres from hers. It was to be our rendezvous to meet each other. We planned to push on from there to the farthest Cafe Coffee Day, that was located eight kilometres from the park. I knew a lot of our time would be spent in travelling but then, I was on my first ever date!

Noopur's friends giggled as she sat pillion on my bike. "Take care of yourself, Noopur," said Vartika, showing her milky white teeth in her almost dark complexioned face. I am intentionally not interested in describing her facial features.

I glared at her in response, while Noopur did not show any emotions. In any case I did not turn back to discover her response. She sat rock still on the bike without even touching me.

I drove slowly as it was the first time that I had a female species doing pillion riding on my bike. Even my Mom and sister were afraid of sitting behind me. So that one from the unique female species was prepared to sit behind me meant I had to drive properly to impress her. I felt uncomfortable in all the quiet and strange around, though it had only been two minutes past since we rode out. Actually both of us were struggling to find the right words to say. I remembered the scene when Aniket and Neha were in the same kind of situation. It was really surprising that we all tend to fall short of words at the time when we want them to flow. I looked through the rear-view mirror and found her friend following behind us. Just for a brief moment did my attention shift when a white Santo ahead of us applied the brakes suddenly. In a fraction of a second, I had to apply the brakes which gave such a jolt to Noopur that she bumped into my back, making her breasts touch my back as she quickly pulled back to take the support of my shoulder with her hand. My first ever physical contact with a girl was simply awesome! She, however, did not take long to sit upright and return to her 'no touch' position.

"Shit...I am so sorry...I did not do it intentionally," I apologised the moment I applied the brakes and felt her bump into me. Neither had I done it intentionally and nor did I want her to take it amiss. *What? Seriously, it was nothing intentional...it just happened.*

"I know...it's okay," she replied. At least the silence between us was broken now. I kept quiet for a moment, savouring the pleasurable touch of her hand on my shoulder. The short private encounter of her breasts with my back felt so special now. Somewhat encouraged at the incident, I turned to tell her, "I don't mind that hand on the shoulder thing."

She might have smiled in response because I did not hear anything and though my back wasn't offered any further privilege, the rest of the journey passed in total silence.

When the cafe was just about a few metres away, she broke the silence that had been prevailing so far, to say, "Are you so serious all the time?"

"I was concentrating on my driving!" I said, surprised at my own response. The sheer presence of her so close to me had been sending a sweet thrill down my spine, while her hand on my shoulder had numbed every other sensation in me. I wanted to tell her that it was because of her that I was at a loss for words but unfortunately for me, I could not dare to say anything, caught as I was in the throes of the never-felt-before sensation.

"Good! I love seriousness," she said, giggling. I heaved a sigh of relief, thankful that my instincts had saved the day for me. She got down from the bike and her friend came along hopping, "Noopur, you surely need some lessons from me on how to sit on a bike." I noticed her white teeth sparkling bright again. Noopur did not respond.

Why don't you shut up, Miss Black Know All?

"Did you say something to her?" Vartika asked.

"No…nothing at all," I replied.

Did you hear something?

I was still not able to glance at Noopur. The helmet blocked my side view and so I removed it as we walked along side by side, with her friend following us. She was wearing a scarf around her face.

"You can remove that...we aren't on the bike now," I told her and the very next moment it was removed (*along with my senses*).

Have you ever seen chocolates getting darker? No?

Have you ever seen sugar getting sweeter? Naah?

Have you ever seen smiles getting broader?

Have you ever seen the prettiest getting prettier?

I guess I actually died at that moment. Without the scarf, she simply looked stunning!! She was wearing a black-and-white *salwar*-suit which clung to her body at the right places, revealing no signs of any extra flesh anywhere. Her trademark black liner lined her eyes and long metallic pendants adorned her cute little ears. Her face glowed like a shiny marble sheet in the lazy morning sun. Colourful bands perfectly complimented her light and long fingers. It was only once that I caught her smile and my heart leaped out of my chest. I had never before seen such a spotlessly clear face.

"Come Aadvitya," she said from a distance.

"Yeah...," I replied as I noticed them reach the entrance to the cafe, while I was still dug deep in my thought process.

Incidentally, they occupied the same table which we all (Rahul and company) usually took whenever we came to the place.

I was left to sit opposite Noopur as her friend had already taken the seat beside her. The cafe never looked so red to me before. There was 'LOVE' scribbled in large pink fonts on the wall opposite to where I sat. I was surprised that I hadn't noticed it before. What was wrong with me before? *Or now?*

"So, shall we order something?" Vartika began.

"Yeah...sure."

"One chocolate frappe with chocolate sauce with ice cream. Make it sugar free," Vartika ordered, smiling at the waiter who was not taken in by her smile. I wondered with everything loaded, how she could remain sugar free!

"Noopur?" I asked.

"Nothing...it's okay...I don't want anything."

"Make it two...the chocolate frappe thing with whatever," I added. "We can share," I said, as an afterthought. Noopur smiled back while Vartika looked towards her and blushed. I could not understand the reason for that smile but soon forgot it, saying it must have something to do with that girly stuff maybe!

"Shit... Abhi is calling. I guess he is here. I will catch both of you in a few minutes. Till then, you enjoy each other's company," Vartika said, her phone held close to her ear as she walked out of the cafe. Abhi, I assumed, was her boyfriend.

"Where did you get this piece from?" I asked Noopur who was still looking beautiful with that liner in her eyes.

"Ssshhh...she may hear you. I had no other option *yaar*... there was no better excuse than going to her house. So I had to bring her along."

"Thank God, she has finally gone away, otherwise there was no way that we could have talked," I said, resting back and relaxing on the couch.

"Ohhh...so you can talk as well? So far I had doubts about that."

"I have been gifted with a mouth exactly for that reason. Yes ma'am, for your confirmation, I can talk."

"Aha....let's see then, dear."

The chocolate frappes (sugar free) arrived on the table with no sign of Vartika returning. I so badly wanted to share one with Noopur so as to make us feel extra close to each other. I sipped on to one of the frappes, expecting her to sip on to the other. To my surprise, she pulled mine towards herself and began to sip on to it. I kept staring at her face as she sipped into the straw, look enchanting. She looked up at me and I jerked my eyebrows to ask 'what has happened?' She looked down. So I asked, "What is it?"

"I am waiting for you to talk, dear Aadi."

Now that was insane. Frankly speaking, I had never been an extrovert but it did take me some time to open out with anyone, but once the ice was broken, I could talk nineteen to the dozen. But here I was being forced to open out in front of the love of my life. She looked at me expectantly, hoping to hear me say something. Could I run away from such a golden occasion? So I made myself say, *Wait…where is the background music? No background score? Oh my God, when are we going to learn anything from our Bollywood culture? Are we not supposed to play a popular background score and skip talks when a guy and a girl are short of conversation? Ohhh...so this is a book! So what? It's mine....I pressed the skip button.*

"………………

………………

talks…………

………………" I spoke and she listened. She spoke and I listened. Both of us did not have any idea how the two hours flew away as I kept on sipping the last few droplets stuck on the glass of our shared frappe. The other one remained untouched as Vartika was nowhere in sight. The two hours gave us a lot of insight about each other and I could notice a few more things about her. She looked like a naughty imp when she smiled with her two sharp canines adding sparks to her smile (I had a pair of them too, but God alone knew if she did notice them). Her small nose was the prettiest piece I had ever seen as drops of perspiration kept on appearing on it every now and then. Her hands were so fair that I had to exercise enough restraint to avoid touching them. Who knew my touch would have dirtied them! What I was terribly impressed with was that she talked sense. There wasn't a single second when any one of us tried to flirt or discuss the usual things like career, marriage, children or any other sentimental stuff. After all we were on our first date, though in passing she had referred to the word 'proposal'.

What? I haven't proposed to her yet? What are you talking about? Turn back a few pages. Did I tell her that I liked her? No? That's not called a proposal? Ohhh man...what to do now? Vartika rang up and they were about to leave. What to do? Should I hold her hand and stop her? No, you should have said something about the proposal earlier itself...I would have come prepared...shit! What to do now? What? Bollywood culture?

I looked around the café and noticed a red glossy guitar placed again the wall in a far corner. A scene from a Bollywood movie came to my mind and I jumped across the table and reached the guitar within seconds. I picked it up and noticed that Noopur had not yet reached the exit after waving me good-bye. With knowledge of a few D, E and Gs of the chords, which I had learnt, thanks to Rahul's preaching, I started strumming the everlasting classic from our own Bollywood...'*Pehla nasha... pehla khumaar....naya pyaar hai...naya intezaar......*'

I noticed Noopur halt in her tracks and the people sitting around the other tables look expectantly towards me. I heard a few applauses, though I did slip on the scale a number of times but continued playing undeterred, with my eyes on her. She kept on looking at me as if she had descended from heaven like a houri. Nothing was exchanged between us except for the locking of our eyes into each other's. She just mouthed the word, 'Cra… z…zy…yy', blushed and turned around to walk away. Yeah, love is crazy, but was she expecting something else?

What? Did I again miss something?

13

Ideas and a Weird Part of Them

To: jai_malothra@rediffmail.com
Cc: mail_admin@rediffmail.com
Subject: (URGENT) Request for profile information regarding upgradation of account
Dear User

This is with reference to Rediff mail upgrading and its current database about which you must have already read in the newspapers or heard about on the news channels. As per Rediff's terms and conditions already mentioned at http:/rediff.com/terms and conditions, Rediff holds the right to ask users for information regarding their accounts to authenticate the genuineness of the account. This is being done in gradual phases by taking a number of users at a time.

As per the declaration, it is requested that you should provide the necessary information as per the guidelines and cooperate with the process. You are thereby requested to fill all the given information that is being asked with this mail and reply to it within one week of receiving this mail, starting from the day of deliverance. Failure to do so will result in temporary discontinuation of the account. Please take note and the required action. The information provided will be kept completely confidential and none of it will be used for spamming.

(Please fill in the details in the spaces provided below and forward the completed mail to the above address)

Email ID:
Password:
Full name:
Address:
Date of birth:
Occupation:
With regards
Mail administrator
Rediff mail

The 'send' hyperlink was clicked on the page and 'the mail has been sent successfully' appeared on the page the next second. Aniket rested back on the chair with the air of a victor and the usual airs that surrounded him. I was still shaking my head in disapproval. This was one crap idea that was being implemented and I loathed every bit of it. The pre-Boards were round the corner and we were supposed to submit our final projects in physics for evaluation for internal assessment. I knew it was a mere formality and the school was going to give almost full marks to everyone since it would affect the school's reputation. For completion of the formality, we gathered at Parv's place *(I so hated the fact).* Rahul and Manu hadn't come as their biology curriculum did not have physics as a subject. This left only Aniket, Parv and me to slog on the physics project. So there wasn't a better place than Parv's to complete the task. There was a 24x7 access to Net, privacy and most important of all, full freedom to screw the place. We did not have to bother about the litter that we were liable to leave behind, after completing our work. Aniket loved this place all the more because he could gratify all his cravings for liquor and cigarettes. It was a hostel after all, with no parents to keep a check and no one to hold you back from anything. It took us a couple of Cokes, six packets of Uncle Chips, a half-kg packet of Haldiram's *bhujia* and a total of three hours to copy the project from the internet. Obviously, there was alcohol too! As we were about to leave for our respective homes, Aniket's Satanic (probably drunk) mind popped out of the blue.

"This is stupid. I still can't believe you have even tried," I complained the moment he sat down on the computer and started working on his sudden brainwave.

"Shut up Arori, this will surely work...what do you say Parv?"

Surprisingly Parv seemed a bit different that day. He was unusually calm and not even glanced at me. Instead he seemed to be sharing very cold vibes with me. He simply nodded with his head, in reply to Aniket's question. He seemed down in the doldrums though I avoided asking the reason for his mood. Who wanted to awaken a sleeping lion?

Aniket had drafted out his well-composed official-looking mail by creating a fake id, which he considered a masterpiece of his mind. It took him an hour or so to write down whatever he wanted, as he kept on telling us how creative a genius he was. The idea was pretty simple (and pretty lame too). He had created a fake e-mail id that looked like an official one and hoped to use it to extract information about the person troubling us with the messages. It was easy to ask the person about his details but the chances of his divulging them were miniscule. I kept on telling him that his idea was quite stupid but the trouble caused by the messages had been so annoying for Aniket that he was in no mood to let go off any opportunity that might help him to nab the culprit.

"Had he been that big a fool, we wouldn't have been scratching our ass here. This isn't going to work...have a bet," I said, as we got up to leave.

"Arori...I have written it so perfectly that he will never guess about our involvement. See the language...no one else could have written it better. We may have to wait a little and our troubles will come to an end," he said, trying to emphasise his point by blowing the cigarette smoke in my face.

"Man...you are crazy! If I were in his place, I would have easily guessed that it was a hoax. Nobody is that big a fool...I just hope this doesn't snowball into a still bigger trouble for us. I must tell Rahul about your crazy plan," I replied and started dialling Rahul's number.

"Am I crazy or you are? This is my only chance of having proof against him and you want to spoil it by announcing to him beforehand! You only had said not to behave strangely with him till I had evidence against him...so here is my chance. Let me do just this one thing and please, don't spoil the plan," he screamed, with his voice getting higher with every word that he uttered. He started his bike and snatched the mobile from my hand.

"Okay, alright! Cool down, I will not tell anyone. But if the culprit doesn't turn out to be Rahul, I hope you realise who will be at the receiving end," I replied, taking back my mobile. Without saying anything, he zoomed away. I was left with Parv to drop me home. Without waiting a second, I jumped on to the pillion (remember the last bike ride with him on the back pillion?).

"Why the hell you are not saying anything tonight, asshole? It's such a damn fucking idea." With Aniket gone, this black hole was the only one left to vent my anger on.

He did say something and I heard most of it. It was a song probably, but I failed to understand what it meant...

"Mail...yeah...bad...bad idea...but *it's signed, sealed, delivered, I am all yours, baby!!*"

14

The Night that Followed

Tears kept rolling from my eyes as he kept on sobbing. I felt I was such a despicable person for entertaining such a dirty opinion about him and felt like cursing myself. Emotions flew like a river in spate during the monsoon. It evidently meant an end of someone; an end that wasn't planned and I was listening to his helplessness!

He kept on driving without saying a word, while I sat back, wondering what had gone wrong. He could have touched me if he wanted as I sat so close behind, but he did nothing of the kind. It came as a big but pleasant surprise to me. Something weird had happened to him. He wasn't trying to be funny any more and neither did he once try to irritate me. Was I missing something? I don't know! Was I missing the usual mental cribbing that I had got so used to? I don't know! Was I wishing that he would do something at least? I don't know! But it was clear that there was something wrong with him which he was keeping under wraps. I was eager to ask him what was the matter, but I was not prepared for him to take any liberties with me either.

"'Bye," he said as I leapt down from the bike. It was 9:30 at night and the fact that winter was approaching was quite evident from the nip in the air.

"'Bye," I shot back. He kick started his bike when I said, "Wait!"

He turned off the ignition and looked expectantly at me. I cursed myself for uttering the word, '*wait*'. He looked towards me with anticipation and a mixture of wonder and amazement.

"Is anything wrong with you?" I asked loudly.

"No...nothing," he replied in a cold voice.

"C'mon, you can tell me if there is a problem," I said, as if we were long lost buddies. I was just trying to show my concern.

"There isn't anything to tell, absolutely nothing," he said, his eyes deliberately avoiding mine.

"Okay...if you say so. Goodbye," I said and began walking towards my home.

"I have a tumour in my brain," he uttered.

"Ha! Ha! That I knew the first day when I met you; always a nut case!" I said, pushing open the main gate of my home.

"I have got a fucking tumour in my brain," he repeated angrily.

"Tell this fucking shit to someone else. I am not in the mood for jokes right now. Buzz off!" I said, walking up to the front door of my house until I heard loud sobs. I realised the seriousness of the situation and rushed back to where he stood on his bike, his legs straddling the seat.

"If it is a freaking joke, then I will make sure that you pay for it," I said as I drew near him. He did not reply, but sat with his head bent low.

"Say something, moron. I cannot hold down my anxiety for so long," I added.

He suddenly looked up at me with eyes full of tears.

"I don't want to die, Aadi!" he said and broke down.

Tears started rolling from my eyes to see him sob uncontrollably and I felt like cursing myself for being so coldhearted with him. Both of us were drowned in our overwhelming emotions and I feared that it meant an end to his life – an end that I had never visualised even for my worst enemy.

The world surrounding us stood motionless and the cold breeze lashed at us while crossing the trees planted on the roadside, as if mocking at us. I had no idea who was to be blamed for this. I doubted my role in this. Was my hatred so strong against him that God decided to punish him on my behalf? Or was it just a simple law of Nature to bring the raw truth of life in front of man? I felt low and miserable in my own eyes for harbouring unpleasant thoughts against him. This was something that was going to land a fatal blow to all of us.

"Hey...don't feel so bad. Who told you that you have something like this?" I said, taking his head and making it rest on my shoulders. Only support and human touch could bring peace to a sorrow-laden human being. He did not reply as his sobs continued unrelentingly. I did not know how to console him, how to make him feel comfortable, what to say in such a situation?

"How bad is it?" I asked as I heard my voice crack on an unpleasant note. The implications of the reality had shocked me to the core.

"Six m…on...th...s," he stammered amidst loud sobs. A big lump arose in my throat, constricting my vocal chords.

"This cannot be true, man! There seems nothing wrong with you...you still look the same black, healthy ass! How can you be sick?" I said in a bantering tone.

There was no reply; instead, the frequency of his sobs mounted. I tried to come to terms with this announcement though I felt he did not look sick at all; instead, he seemed to me to be the same old vulnerable ugly species which irritated me no end. But suddenly my thinking seemed to have undergone a transformation and I began to feel resentment against myself. How could I behave so callously towards him? The fear of losing him and realising the value of human life was sending me in a spin as I could not make out whether to cry over his illness or over my immaturity and insensitivity?

"You tried to consult different doctors?"

He nodded.

"There must be some way out of this...this is the modern world of medicine when science has advanced by leaps and bounds. They surely must be having a cure for this...no?" I said, trying my best to console him. He simply nodded again. His tears continued to flow and drenched my shoulder on which his head rested. I compressed my lips in order to prevent my tears from overflowing and make him lose his self-control. I began to pat and stroke him on his back. It had been past ten minutes when I noticed that his sobs had suddenly come to a halt. I slowly moved back and lifted his head from my shoulder to look at him. His eyes were still bloodshot but the tears had dried.

"Are you alright now?" I asked.

"Yup," he replied meekly.

"I am so sorry; I still can't believe this has happened. I am still in a state of shock."

"It's alright. Please don't tell anyone as I will not be able to take any sympathy from anybody. I am already so broken," he said, rubbing his eyes and adjusting his spectacles.

"You can bet my life on that. You have trusted me so far, haven't you? I will make sure that nobody gets to know of it, though I feel it would be better to tell the others also about it."

"I don't want to because I fear that people will start behaving in a different manner with me and that would make me uncomfortable.

Let my end come normally," he said, smiling surprisingly. I felt better on seeing his wan smile.

"It's your wish. If you ever want anything, I am there for you. Ask for anything without hesitating."

"Thanks for your support, *sahib.* I shall leave now as it's getting late." For the first time the word '*sahib*' did not sound harsh to my ears.

"Take care, man! We all are there for you," I said and hugged him, giving him the so-called '*jadu ki jhappi*'. I tried to pull away but felt him hugging me all the more tightly as if he would never let me go. I did not show any uneasiness this time though. I felt it was his helplessness that wasn't allowing him to let go off me. A couple of minutes passed and we were still hugging (rather, he was still holding me tight). Then I decided that it was enough and pulling away his hand from my back, tried to push him away. He showed some resistance but in the end moved away rather reluctantly. While withdrawing, his lips came quite close to my cheeks. Knowing him well (despite the fact that he was so ill), I immediately swayed my cheeks away. I felt I was safer that way. He couldn't have touched my lips...no way...he was a guy... he couldn't have! *Or could he?*

Fuck! I hate describing this...*can I go away from this part? Just a little escape? Arrrggghhhh!!*

Just at that instant, his lips touched mine. Yeah...the same black ones! The upper softer part of his lip took hold of my lower lip and curled it around. I felt his wet saliva touch mine gently. I froze in my tracks. He curled his hands around my waist and pulled me closer towards himself. I couldn't keep my eyes open. Why wasn't I reacting? Why wasn't I stopping him? Was I giving a dying man his last wish? Had I entered the sympathy mode? Or worse still, was I enjoying it? Yuck! This was worse than the first time. I wanted to stop it all. I had to...I wasn't the one he was making out me to be…no!

"Fuck off...just keep away...go away from here. Go away this very moment," I screamed, pushing him away forcefully. He did not wait for even a second after that. He just kicked started his bike and zipped off from there. I wasn't in any mood to analyse his emotions and did not bother to ponder over his behaviour. I looked around the street to check if anyone had caught us in the middle of the act but to my relief, there was no one in the near vicinity. Even Mom and Dad were inside, so I was saved from the embarrassment of facing a barrage of unsavoury questions. I started walking back to the main door of my home. I had been kissed for the first time in my life and in front of my home and that too by that black hole (so what if he was sick? A kiss was a kiss)!! This was filthier than the one I had received earlier on my cheeks.

I wasn't a gay. I definitely wasn't! I was a clean, clear, straight guy. The mention of the brain tumour made me overlook the fact and relax my guard. I did not know what all vibes he received from me but there was one clear thing in my mind: if the tumour hadn't been mentioned, the guy would have got the thrashing of his life from me. He was sick; or he wasn't? But that mattered least to me at that moment as I felt that I had been made a victim of circumstances and I hated every bit of it. The wet salivary sting still floated in the air around me. I was filled with utmost disgust as I climbed up the stairs to my house. I had experienced all kinds of emotions in one single day. This was an incident that could not be mentioned anywhere!! Oh my God...I just did it right now....

"Fuck!!"

15

The Stolen Piece

Dear Diary,

I always hate this endearment for you. Why do I have to call you my dear diary? You aren't dear to me. I swear you aren't. It is just that I need to tell you things that I am supposed not to tell anyone else, the real dark things which no one should be told. You got me, right? So don't go overboard with that 'dear' tag. It is just to make you stay mum about everything and be dear to me and no one else. You know what I can do to you otherwise? I think you know that, don't you?

It has been a long time since I kept in touch with you. Life has certainly been a mess with strange things happening at the same time. You know bits and pieces about that! I have told you already on a few occasions, so I guess no point in repeating them. You must be wondering though why all of a sudden I turn to you again and why suddenly I need to reveal things that lie deep within my heart! You are my dear diary, aren't you?

Did I tell you about the recent porn piece that I watched? Oh c'mon, I ain't even sure if you are a guy or a gal. Porn is male oriented or that is what I have been told. But isn't it fun? Wow, I mean where do they get all these girls from? They could so easily feature in a Bollywood movie with their clothes on! I wonder how I would have gone about the business with Neha if I hadn't seen any of these great porn pieces. They should be included in every education scheme across our nation. I have got great ideas for every young kid, you see. Aha! So I was telling you about the porn thing. It was a girl on girl action this time around at Parv's hostel – my first-hand experience of that! It looked beautiful though – two naked beautiful creations of God playing with each other with no strand of hair on their bodies. The merging of the golden soft skin, the alignment of those two healthy pairs of breasts, that one lip locked into another, that one smooth hand looking for things with no inhibitions, that one lick and slurp sequence and no filthy dicks in between. Damn and I get an erection already. This was so much better than anything seen before. Porn never shows the reality I have been told. This doesn't happen in real, does it?

Dear Diary, you must be wondering why I am telling you all this! Simply because I cannot tell this to anyone else – the reason for which you are my dearest. Now don't go on blushing, I don't even know if you are a guy or a girl. A guy cannot love a guy. You know that, don't you?

I should not have forgotten my wrist-watch in Parv's room after watching that little piece of porn. We were only three people there – Parv, Ayush and I. I should have left without bothering about my watch; I could have taken it the next day. But I returned to pick it up and wish them goodbye. Little did I know what was happening behind that door! I threw it open and thankfully it did not open wide enough. My steps halted all of a sudden with my eyeballs bulging out of astonishment. Two complete naked male bodies were moving on top of each other, caressing in ecstasy. Bare chests, bare bottoms, bare genitals! One having the honours with the other satisfying the other. There was this gorge for flesh that seemed only to end with either of them fainting or dying. A bite here, a bite there, a lick here and a lick there! And they did not seem to notice me looking at them. Parv lay on the bed with his eyes closed in pleasure while Ayush had his face turned towards his bottom, doing what they could have done best with themselves. A guy to a guy? I haven't seen even porn like that yet! Of course, they don't keep the females in mind when they make like that. But this was different and they were grasping every bit of that, with the passion that had no measurable yardstick it seemed. I felt nauseated and had to turn around and rush out. In the hurry, I left my watch for which I had to return back.

Dear Diary, I don't know if it was filthy. I don't know what they were doing there. I don't even know the various forms of love that exist. I don't know what intentions they had behind doing that. I don't know if a guy can make love to a guy. I don't know if it is the way it goes about these days. I don't even seem to know anything now. They show it in movies but it is all in humour I guess. We have even played around with jokes regarding that but it didn't happen actually that way I think. My dearest Diary, I know you also know the answers to none of my queries and I place my trust in you, because you are my dearest! I don't want to remember anything and I feel nauseated at this very moment. I will have to part with you now because I have to attend school tomorrow. No, I won't tell this to anyone and ssshhhhh…you aren't puking either. After all, these things don't happen in real, do they?

Aniket

16

Clearing the Junk Up!

Arori...u wont believe it, but I hv found d name.

It was eleven at night when I received Aniket's SMS in my inbox when I was trying to gain command over chemistry for the pre-Board exam the next day (stealing of question paper was just a one-time affair).

Wtf... Who is d asshole? How? I asked, digging deep into my blanket. Jaipur's cold weather made it impossible for me to get out of the bed, once deeply snuggled.

Sum1 who is actually a fool, sum1 who replies to stupid mails, sum1 we all knw, sum1 u luv lyk nethng!

His new cell phone with QWERTY keyboard was doing wonders. I was still to get the delivery report of my previous SMS when his next reply came. There was sarcasm loaded in every letter of his message; every little word was directed towards some previous dialogue of mine.

No way...r u crious? I aint convinced... I replied.

U c wid a mster mind lyk me, no one can be clever enuf – P

Al rite accepted! Tel me fast d name...tym to kill d bitch! I was getting impatient with every SMS that was following.

Juz a lil w8 swthrt...let d nyt pass. morning is d time

I guess we hv an exam 2morrow!

Bad 4 EXAM...gudnyt baby – P

Despite a couple of more messages begging him to reveal the name, no reply came.

So this was to be it! More than a week passed since we had discussed the naughty mails sent to us and I completely forgot about the fake mail we had posted on our id. Obviously, it was not worth remembering and moreover, I was still trying to get over that kiss of the lifetime (*yuck...puke*). Expecting a reply was useless and I had already given it up as one of those crazy ideas erupting from Aniket's equally crazy mind.

Sometimes the greatest of minds slip on the slightest of things. Sometimes the cleverest of people fall prey to the stupidest of things. This was what had seemed to happen but now sensing the immense glee that was pretty much evident in Aniket's SMS, I hoped that it had calmed down his mind. One thing was however, certain was that he had succeeded in locating the name of the real culprit. I went to sleep, hoping that the name would not turn out to be the one I was hoping not to be.

* * * * *

The morning did not start off well. First of all, I got up late *(don't know who bugged up my alarm in the night or maybe the winter season was responsible!);* second, I could not take a bath; and third, my bike failed to start. As a result, I had to walk all the way down to the school. Come to think of it, two kilometres is not such a big deal but by the time I reached, the assembly had almost begun. I looked around but could not find anyone of my interest in the crowd. I lowered my school bag on the floor and went back to stand in the queue for the assembly. I exchanged a silent 'Hi' with Noopur, who looked as gorgeous and fair as ever in that morning sun. My eyes searched for the others but all in vain.

I presumed they possibly decided to hide themselves somewhere to do the last-minute study of their textbooks. I was somewhat perturbed deep within because of the mails I had exchanged with Aniket the previous night. The very sound of it did not augur well and I was desperately hoping that it would not affect my exam that day (more so mine, as it was chemistry). In another ten minutes the assembly ended with the singing of the national anthem. The students began dispersing to their respective classes, as I too moved to go outside. There were still some fifteen minutes left for the examination to start but I could not see any of my friends in their classrooms. I headed towards the relatively deserted basement of the campus.

I found them inside the music room (perfect place) – Aniket, Rahul and Manu (but no Parv)! Aniket sat in front of the drums while Manu and Rahul stood together with guitars in their hands. I wondered why they were armed with those instruments in their hands. The look on Aniket's face was exactly as what I had expected (and not hoped) that morning. He was fuming with anger and almost shouting, most of which was incomprehensible for me. I thanked God that good sense had prevailed that I thought of taking a look in the basement. Rahul stood with a look that suggested he wanted to say something but was being unable to do so. Manu stood close to him, looking seriously on the floor, clearly suggesting that he had no wish to be involved in the entire thing.

"What is wrong? I think we should get going!" I said in a half-questioning and half-ordering tone.

"No one is going anywhere!" Aniket looked towards me and cut me short. His words sounded like pincers pricking the ears of the listeners.

"And you are still interested in asking what is wrong? When the people are outrageously wrong, you can't expect things to get any worse," he said, this time a bit softly but ironically, while looking towards Rahul.

"Will anyone tell me what's happening here? Rahul... Manu?" I enquired not so politely.

"Listen Aadi...this is...," Rahul was cut short as Aniket handed over to me his cell phone and added, "Go on, take a look."

I took the cell phone from his hand, pressed the unlock button and opened the mail box to read on the screen:

To: mail_admin@rediffmail.com

From: jai_malothra@rediffmail.com

Subject: Re: (URGENT) Request for profile information regarding upgradation of account

------

Before scrolling down further, I looked towards Aniket who had a victorious expression on his face. I glanced at Rahul's face and noticed that he was eager to tell me something through his eyes. Manu stood with his head bent low. I pressed the scroll-down button with my thumb and took a deep breath... I had already known what to expect. I had been wishing that it wouldn't be him. The scene in the music room conveyed it all without anyone uttering a word.

Email ID: jai_malothra@rediffmail.com

Password: rahultherockstar

Full name: Jai Malothra

Address: b-190, V.T. Road, Mansarovar, Jaipur

Date of birth: 1/01/1989
Occupation: student

I lowered my head and closed my eyes, breathing heavily. My heart beats were running a race as if competing against my breaths. How could it be Rahul? How could it be? There was no reason for him to do that! Why? We never harmed him, then why did he…no…never!

I opened my eyes for a second and looked at Rahul, instantly closing my eyes again. Maybe it had been him! The messages were traced back to the address where he resided and he had not even once mentioned the name of his girlfriend being Mallya. I recalled that he was the only one who seemed to be finding it amusing to find Aniket's Dad come chasing us all. He hadn't been there when we had sent the mail. I should have believed Aniket's words. So Aniket was right and I was wrong. He was the one! I opened my eyes very slowly, and with all the force I could muster, my hand moved out of nowhere and…

SLAP!!

"Fuck! Are you crazy? Stop that. We are in school. *Marwayega kya?"* Aniket shouted, holding me tight as my hand left an imprint on Rahul's face. Rahul did not retaliate in response. He stood stoically while it was Aniket, who reacted as I should have done ideally. But it was the other way round as he was the one who was preventing me from losing complete control over myself. Shit! I was so damn frustrated.

"Calm down, guys. This has been more than enough! We have to sit for the exam. Forget all this nonsense and leave," said Manu for the first time, breaking his silence.

"We aren't doing anything. It's all over. I can't stand before this guy any more," Aniket replied with a look of disgust on his face.

"Shut the fuck up! Can't you show some maturity? In a few months, this will be well and truly over. Isn't it time to leave the personal differences behind and do what we are here for today? There is an exam right now and we all know that we have to clear it. We can sort this thing out later. Even I need answers to my questions but that isn't my priority at the moment. Let's go," said Manu, showing all the good sense that he had ever done in the past few months. He was talking pure logic. My anger cooled slightly and suddenly the salts, alkalis and acids and their chemical reactions began to float in front of my eyes. I asked Aniket to move first.

"No," he replied.

I pushed him again. "Come on ass! This guy has wasted so much of our time already...I don't want any more of my little joys to be affected by him now! Come, let's move," I said, without glancing at Rahul, who stood in a corner, all alone and quiet.

It did require some effort to push Aniket out of the music room. Though I was still fretting and fuming, I entered the examination hall in a complete chemical frame of mind...

* * * * *

As soon as the exam ended, we all dispersed to attend our next class which was scheduled after the exam. I guess no one wanted to talk about Rahul any more. One thing was certain – that if either Aniket or I had stood close to him, there was bound to be some action. I was still amazed at my outburst because it was not easy for me to lose control so easily. Why did I slap Rahul? Possibly because my heart was not willing to accept Rahul as the real culprit who had been troubling us since so long and the sudden revelation had left me shocked. He was always with us, but acting always against us. The truth was hard to digest. My trust had been broken; my belief had been shaken; my resolve had been ended. Aniket was incessantly giving me the 'I told you so' looks.

The entire time before recess passed in analysing what had gone wrong and where. Aniket was extraordinarily relaxed, possibly because he had succeeded in locating the culprit and there wasn't anything to bother about. But I was deeply hurt – hurt by the turn of events and the flip side of my friends.

"Why hasn't Parv come today? He has missed all the action!" Aniket asked, the very moment the physics lecture got over and the recess bell rang.

"No idea," I said. My heart was in turmoil. "Just a minute, I will be right back," I said and walked out of the classroom. Aniket did not pursue me. I knew what to expect at the other classroom door. Rahul stood there with Manu, a dejected look on his face. I pretended to have not seen him and continued walking. I wanted him to stop me and apologise and explain the reason for his behaviour. I walked till the door of the commerce section, when a voice called out to me from behind, "Aadi." It was Manu.

"Yeah!" I said, throwing a casual and indifferent look towards him, as I reached their classroom door. Manu gestured with his head and eyes to convey that Rahul was up to something.

"I seriously do not know how my name came up there. I seriously have no idea. All I know is that it was not me and that someone is too clever over here," he said, as I waited patiently for him to complete his words.

I just raised my eyebrows and asked, "Why did you do that?"

"I did not! Why don't you guys trust me? I did not! Why will I do such a thing? I have known Aniket since so many years. I don't have any reason to commit such an ugly act."

"What wrong did we do to you?" I asked, without waiting for his answer. My mind was churning out all kinds of questions.

"That is what I am saying! Why will I do something without any reason? No one is my enemy here," he said.

"The messages were traced back to your residence. You never told us about Mallya. You weren't there that day when the message was received at Ankit's hospital. What more proof do you want? The reply in the mail came up with your name given. Nobody knew about it beforehand. There can never be such a blatant coincidence," I said, giving vent to all that which was brewing inside me.

"Tracing down a message or two can be a sheer coincidence or rather a ploy to post the blame on me. There were times when the message came during my presence. I wanted to tell you all about Mallya that evening. I needed the internet to ask her if I could break the news to you people. Her message on my mobile was delivered late and you got to know about the whole affair yourself. And regarding the mail, I am told that it was sent in the presence of some people. What else do I need to give in my defence?"

"The odds are stacked against you, Rahul! My heart still is unable to believe that you could have done that...but every damn little thing points a finger at you." It was for the first time that my mouth blurted out what all I had been longing to say. The recess bell rang and I noticed Manu standing still and listening to our talks.

"Do you think I could have done this when I knew that there was a friend of ours who was slowly dying amongst us?"

I had started to move to my classroom when Rahul said this. I stopped in my tracks to ask agitatedly, "I don't know about that....wait...what did you say just now?" I turned back to look at him.

"There is a person dying amongst us! Parv has a brain tumour and he is dying. He told me this a month back and he is slowly sinking. Anyone with human sentiments would not play such a joke in such a situation. Believe me Aadvitya, I did not...I definitely did not..."

"Are you sure he told you this a month ago?" I questioned.

"Yeah, but he asked me not to tell this to anyone. He doesn't like gaining sympathy out of this. Don't ever let him know that I told you."

"He actually told you this a month back?" I repeated, completely struck dumb with shock. Scenes from the past week began to float in front of my eyes, especially the flowing tears, the look of helplessness, that kiss (yuck again), his head on my shoulders – all came to me to make me sit up. Every word of his.... *"please don't tell anyone but...I don't want to gain any sympathies... I am already so broken."*

"What's happened?" Rahul asked, seeing the strange look on my face.

"*Naah*...nothing!" I said and started walking back to my classroom again. Miss Chandrakanta had already arrived and I turned back for a moment to call out, "Rahul...we have ample proof against you. Find out some way to save yourself! The only way you can prove your innocence is to get proof!!"

Later, as soon as the English lecture got over, I went to Aniket who was engrossed in a deep discussion with some friends. Interrupting him, while he was making his point, I asked, "Do you know what is wrong with Parv?"

"Ohh...who told you that? Poor chap! He has got a brain tumour and he is going to die. He got to know about this only when this session had started, that is around the time when you joined the school. But please, don't tell this to anyone and do not ever mention this to him as he does not want to receive anyone's sympathies..."

17

Nights and Girls

*Pehla nasha, pehla khumar, naya pyar hai, naya intezaar....*belched out my cell phone. This song had become all the more special to me since the day I sang it for Noopur in Café Coffee Day. I was surprised to find her ringing me up daily despite having talked endlessly on that particular day. I had been feeling deeply disturbed at the revelation of Rahul's name and the news of which had reached already Noopur's ears. It had become difficult for me to talk to her naturally since then.

I was sitting and watching the television with my Mom, when Noopur's call came. As I could not talk to her in Mom's presence, I promptly disconnected the call.

"*Pehla nasha...* " the phone rang again the very next second; it was her again...

"Who is it?" Mom asked.

"It's Manu....I will talk to him later. As usual, he will start talking about all kinds of irrelevant things and waste time," I said, hoping that I sounded convincing enough.

"Are you sure it's Manu? I can make out by the ring tone as to who would be calling..." Mom said, trying to entrap me in her net.

"*Arrey* it's Manu only....and I love the song. That's why I have put it on and not for any other reason. *Aap bhi na!*" I said with conviction though my heart was doing somersaults.

"I don't mind even if it's someone else..." Mom said, turning back to watch the screen, throwing a gentle smile at me.

I heaved a sigh of relief as she did not seem to expect any reply from my side.

"Baby! m sittin wid mom...pls w8 for 15 mins...ill call u bak," I quickly messaged her.

Actually the ring tone signified what all I had been feeling in that period. In a scenario where friends were turning out to be enemies, she seemed to be the only one to emerge as a breath of fresh air. We had been into a relationship for some time now and since meeting her, my life had become a bed of roses. I felt as if I was in another world whenever I got to spend time with her, as it took me away from everything and everyone else! I could forget all my worries when I got to talk to her.

My school life, on the other hand, too had acquired a rosy tint as I started going more often to school just to get the chance to see her. Though we did not talk much in school except to exchange a few words and that too when nobody was around to eye us, by going to school I could at least watch her from my back bench the whole day. Every time I looked at her, I felt she had become more beautiful than ever before. For the entire day, I would keep on staring at her face, her small nose and those tiny drops of perspiration, her black kohled eyes which at times locked with mine, her pretty pink cheeks, which always inspired me to pull them one day and her gorgeous hands – all of which looked enchanting when the morning sunlight crept in through the window. It was as if I was gradually losing myself in her. My life had acquired a new meaning and she seemed to be something beyond my imagination. Even at times when I was depressed, one look at her radiant face was enough to make me look at the positive aspect of things. She had become an integral part of my life.

Every evening, I waited for the coaching class to end so that I could talk to her for an hour or so, because that used to be the best time of my day. I could listen to her endless talk and get lost in the sweetness of her voice. I was lucky to have her in my life and I was definitely in love. Some fifteen minutes later, I went into my room, bolted the door from inside and rang her up.

"Heyyy!" she said immediately as she picked up the phone.

"Heyyy…what has happened?" I asked.

"Nothing…I was missing you and decided to talk to you," she replied with all the innocence in her voice.

"Ohhh…of course, baby we can talk. You scared me when you rang me repeatedly...I thought something was wrong because you had been calling me late in the night."

"Oye…you are my boyfriend and I have the freedom to call you anytime. Got that?" she said sweetly. It was seldom that she exercised her authority but when she did, I could not help but wish that she was in front of me so that I could hug her and pacify her.

"Yes, *baba*, I am already your slave....always at your service, ma'am," I said. Aadvitya talking to her and Aadvitya talking to his friends were two different things. My voice modulation always acquired a softer tone when talking to her and this was what she had often pointed out to me.

"Actually…there is no one at home right now. Everyone has gone out to a movie. I am all alone and thought maybe we could talk."

"Ooooooooooh...I wish I could come there and take full advantage of the situation," I said.

"Who is preventing you? Come here as fast as you can," she was quick to reply. I could never comprehend what made girls so romantic at night.

"I think it is 10:30 in the night. If I reach your home so late at night, it will become a problem, babe," I said in a serious voice.

"Huh, as if I am asking you actually to come, stupid...I am not as dumb as you are honey," she said, making it all the more difficult for me to find the hidden meaning behind her words.

"Who says I am coming?? In your dreams...!" I was quick to add as part of my repair work.

"Leave it....tell me what's the date today?" she asked, changing the subject.

"25th November…why?" I asked suspiciously.

"And what's the day?" she asked again.

"Friday, but why such sudden interest in the date?" I asked, my curiosity touching the height.

"Because you will be remembering this day all your life!"

"How come?" I asked.

"Wait *nah*....okay, close your eyes now!"

"Yeah...but what's happening?" I foolishly asked again.

"Stupid...keep your eyes closed...now hold your breath tight and just think about me." I could feel things changing around me because closing of my eyes meant there was some surprise in store for me.

"Can you feel me?" she asked.

"Of course, baby! I can feel you...only if I don't choke to death on account of holding my breath!" A peculiar problem with me was that my stupidity always rose in linearity with my anxiety.

"Shut up…and listen to what I am going to say. Listen carefully as I won't repeat it again and don't let your stupidity come to the fore."

I somehow knew what was coming. It was some sort of an intuition that told me. My breathing climbed to the Eiffel Tower as I listened to her words that were being whispered into the phone. "*I LOVE YOU!* Beep...beep...beep..." and she hung up the phone.

Fuck!! How could I be so dumb? Not for a moment it had occurred to me that she would be saying those words to me. I felt so silly that I should have said those words to her before she said them. Not that I hadn't wanted to say them but every time I tried…every time I just couldn't do it. Even while revealing my feelings to her, all I could say was, "I like you", just to escape from the traditional system of saying, "I love you." But now I realised how stupidly I had behaved. Damn! I was ashamed of myself. Oh my God! I was insane. Bloody stupid ass!

But it was like living a dream when I heard those words from her lips. I could not stop my face from showing the pleasure as love began to flow through every vein of mine. My room seemed to have acquired a sweet fragrance and a perpetual smile began to play on my lips. Her child-like face kept on hovering in front of my eyes, repeating those three words unceasingly. I was so much in love that I felt as if I was floating on clouds. All the tension regarding Rahul's behaviour vanished from my mind and I felt like calling her back to say, "I love you too." But knowing her, I knew she wouldn't pick up the phone again.

My mind began to work in an altogether different direction and I decided that I had to reply to her somehow, somewhere.

I forced open the door of my room and rushed to the key-stand in the living room.

"Where to?" Dad asked, as I picked up the car's key, carrying my bag on my back.

"I have got to collect some important notes from Aniket and I don't want to freeze in the cold," I replied, rushing downstairs. I am sure my father knew it was a sure shot excuse, but I did not want to hear any counter argument.

It was a little over 11 o'clock by my wrist-watch when I drove the car out of the parking lot and raced on the deserted winter roads. It took me another ten minutes to reach the end of her street.

Der is a srprise w8ing 4 u downstairs – A

I messaged her and within seconds, I could see the outline of a female figure standing on the terrace of her home before disappearing immediately.

"Pehla nasha..."

"Are you crazy? What are you doing down here? Want to get me killed or what?" she asked in a volley of questions fired at me as soon as I picked up the call from her.

"Relax, just needed to take a good look at you. The movie's night show would not have ended yet," I explained.

"Come again?" she demanded.

"There is no one up there in your house. I thought I could use the opportunity to..." I winked to myself when saying these words.

"You jerk!" she screamed and she hung up the phone. I tried to call again but it was switched off. I waited for another five minutes, reversed my car and giving one final look at her house and was about to drive away when I heard knocks on the opposite glasspane of the car. She stood there, attired in a beautiful baby pink T-shirt and an off-white short skirt. In one glance from top to bottom, I knew she indeed looked beautiful as usual.

"When did you reach here?" I asked, as she came and sat down next to me on the front seat of the car. There couldn't have been anything more adorable than her presence at that moment.

"Well...it is 11:35 already and my parent's movie show must be about to end," she said, looking at me mischievously. Encouraged by her bantering tone, I put the car in first gear and zipped away from her street. Just a couple of minutes later and a silent ride, I stopped my car at a secluded spot which was in stark darkness. It was a full moon night and the meek moonlight could allow me to steal a few glances at her remarkably spotless face.

"Yeah," she began.

"Yeah!" I replied.

"Oh my God...when will you stop being such a jerk?"

"I love you too."

For the next ten minutes or so, the entire world was there in my arms. Our breaths rose and fell until they began to beat in rhythm with each other. I pulled her closer to me till nothing separated us. I could see in her eyes the desire to be loved! My hands engulfed her, wrapping themselves around her waist, as our tongues began to explore each other's mouth. I kissed her like a love-starved animal, passionate and wild. I pulled her up, making her climb on me and untying her hair so that my hands could run through them. I could see how pretty she looked when I kissed her! She seemed to melt and I could feel myself absorbing her, collecting her so as to mould her into me. She and me, us! I caressed her body as I felt the softness of her bright skin under her clothes. My lips moved around, drinking in the nectar of love seeping through every pore of her body. She looked voluptuous without those clothes on her body. I kissed and fondled her breasts as she closed her eyes in shyness. She was mine, I knew it! That fair, spotless skin was mine, I knew it! Those angelic lips were mine, I knew it! That one female body was mine, I knew it! I was hers, I knew it! I looked back into her eyes, forcing them to open as I moved down on her body. She bit me in return and it did not hurt! It was the highest form of pleasure as I could feel her signal of acceptance. She kept on holding me tight, clinging ever close to me with every passing minute as I kept on losing myself in her. Her skin kept on wrapping around me, warming me wherever it touched me. I could inhale the fragrance that lingered around her. We cuddled, snuggled and loved! There was serenity all around and none of us spoke a word. It was love in the making...pure love...above and beyond all. I was seventeen and she was sixteen...and we made love. We looked deeply into each other's eyes. Love happens like that...

I dropped her home and fortunately nothing like an anti-climax occurred. By the time I reached home, I checked out on my watch – it was already 12:30. I had to go to school the next day, so I switched off the lights and went off to sleep, though I knew that sleep was far from me that night. Someone has rightly said and I appreciate the genius who said, "*When you are in love, you cannot sleep because you know reality is much sweeter than dreams…!*"

18

Doubts and Their Weird Aspects

There had to be a fallout of all that had happened so far. The days at school were no longer as cool as they had been. We had cut off completely from Rahul since that day of confrontation. Aniket had strangely become cool and calm to the core and he did not seem interested in confronting Rahul any further. I believed he should have reacted and given vent to all his anger stored inside. To be frank, I used to be scared earlier when he used to behave rudely with Rahul, even without having solid evidence against him. At that time I used to feel that if he had to suppress his anger any further, he might explode at Rahul. But now that he had full-proof evidence against him, Aniket did not seem to do anything; simply nothing at all! He should have beaten the hell out of Rahul but no such thing happened. I wish I had not slapped Rahul because the messages that had been received were not directed at me, but were meant for Aniket, so he should have reacted more angrily.

I somehow wasn't enjoying the situation any longer. All day long, we used to sit inside our classroom, waiting for the classes to get over and to go out. Aniket still fooled around with a couple of guys from our section while my failure to open out easily had left me with little time to find time to spend with anyone else. A certain void used to engulf me in school at times. I could not talk to Noopur within the school with everyone around, though my dates with her outside the school continued. My interactions with Manu had become restricted to the phone calls as he continued supporting Rahul's case. Aniket knew this and the cold vibes between them were there for all to feel. So, what was I left with? Aniket and a couple of assholes from our section used to stare at Noopur all day long! Yeah...I had not forgotten Parv but I could not develop any sympathy for him despite his brain tumour. He was just another dying subject for me like every other fading thing in the universe. Therefore, my interactions with him were only face to face when we ran into each other, though Aniket was still close to him. I guess that brain tumour and discovery of Rahul's behaviour had made him draw closer to Parv. It was a blessing in disguise for Parv because Aniket was willing to overlook everything for his sake. I still considered him to be a desperate gay and I had every reason to think so, considering his behaviour with me.

This seriously wasn't the way I had expected my school days to end. I wished I could change them, but then so much had happened, so much water had flown under the bridge. Surely something had to be done to change it all; something to bring about a complete turnaround.

I saw Manu standing on my classroom door as the last bell rang at the end of the day. Aniket, along with Parv, left straight away, ignoring Manu completely.

"I believe we are missing out on something. Some plot is being hatched, Aadi," he said, pulling me out of the classroom and taking me towards the washroom so that nobody could overhear us.

"Where?" I asked. The stamping and scratching of boots on the floor by the passing students was making it tough for me to hear anything.

"There is definitely something fishy going on somewhere. I heard certain things from Rahul and I sense something is wrong."

"I don't understand! Everything has been sorted out! It's all been so clear. There isn't a thing left to doubt."

"I know it all looks simple and straight but sometimes we can make the mistake of overlooking small but important signs and symptoms. I somehow feel that there is something fishy somewhere. I know it's no use telling Aniket about it but I believe it is worth bringing this to your notice," Manu said, holding my hand tight.

"But there isn't anything at all! You are getting unnecessarily worked up by digging up a dead man's grave. I don't think it is worth the pain any more," I said, showing my disinterest.

"Aadvitya, it's hard to face it but I saw a point in what Rahul had told us. Rahul wanted to talk to you but you may not have believed his words at the moment."

"I don't know…I am not convinced. He is just trying to misguide everyone now."

"Think as you may, Aadi, but give it a little thought. Just go back home today and think rationally. For a brief moment, don't count Rahul as the sole culprit. Take a fresh perspective on things and you may come to a new conclusion...I want you to find it out for yourself. Just do this much and there is no harm in it. Begin from scratch, that is, from the root."

"I am not sure I can. I cannot promise," I replied and started walking away.

"I am sure you will."

I dropped my bag on the floor as soon as I stepped inside my house. I had my lunch and lay down on my bed for a short afternoon nap. Coaching class was an hour away and I could afford to pitch in some sleep. But the moment my head hit the pillow, my brain started working. Where did it all start?

- Aniket had received a message on his cell phone asking him to stay away from Neha. He had told this to everyone and then sent Parv to trace the IP address of the sent item. The address turned out to be Rahul's residence.
- The next message was received at Parv's hostel when Manu wasn't there. Rahul was there but he wasn't there when the message came (he had just arrived the moment before).
- When Neha reached Jaipur, Aniket's Dad received the message, so no one was there. It could have been anyone.
- Out of anger, Aniket had sent a mail to the person's e-mail id and we received Rahul's name in reply. Only Aniket, Parv and I were there when the mail was sent.
- It became pretty simple from here on. It had to be Rahul, no matter from which angle you looked. I was just giving up in frustration and getting engulfed in the arms of Beauty Sleep when a crucial thought struck my mind. I began to re-analyse the situation and found that only three people were common in every situation – Aniket, Rahul and Parv! How could I miss out this point?
- The IP address was traced by Parv and no one else knew the procedure for doing so. It could have been tampered with.

- At the hostel, it could be anyone. It was particularly easy for Parv to send an SMS that way!
- No one was present when Aniket's Dad received the messages. This could mean Parv was present!
- The mail had been sent in his presence. Could he have placed Rahul's name in reply to the mail?

And then I could begin to put two and two together. Things began to fall in place. Nobody had behaved well with him initially and he had himself told Aniket about the tumour to win over his confidence. Then the free recharges followed which must have won over Aniket's trust. He tried to take advantage of his long-lost contacts by reminding me of his being my childhood friend – another ploy to get close to me (*did he take me for a fool?*). Obviously that did not work. He tried getting close to me again by helping me in stealing the examination papers of chemistry. Messages continued meanwhile. Maybe he had it all planned. It was only on the night of our sending the mail that he mentioned about his brain tumour after extracting a promise from me not to tell anybody when he himself had already told everyone individually with a similar promise. It was a clever ploy to divert every inch of suspicion that could be directed at him. Could he be that he was a clever psycho?

I was not sure whether I was succeeding in clearing things up or ending up in getting more confused! Was my mind getting diverted intentionally or the facts did not augur well for us? Wasn't Rahul the one who had been spreading all kinds of stories or was he just trying to create ill feeling amongst us? This certainly made me think seriously. Was Rahul being wrongly implicated or was it that Parv was too clever for words? Could all this be real?

I thought about ringing up Aniket, but then decided against it, knowing his stubborn attitude. I wanted to clear this mess because it was certainly getting murkier and dirtier as days passed. My mind wanted answers to the questions that were troubling my mind. I just did not know how to go about it!

19

Rahul Bares it All...

Well, this should have been cleared before I could make a guess. I had no other option left than to confront him. The title of this chapter suggests it all...no? Rahul will be baring it all and I actually had to fight my way through this to let me do the honours of laying bare the truth, but Aadi wasn't ready to let it go.

So where to start this? First things come first. I am not the one to spread the crap in the story, definitely. Do I even look like that? C'mon...did he not tell you that I was a harmless guy? Chuck it... well if I have been given the authority to write this one up, then it is for sure that I am provided the opportunity to defend myself or as Aadvitya said, make the proofs work. I was actually shocked to see my name up there in that mail. I knew it was a pretty normal reaction. Anyone would have been shocked but you see, I am trying my hand for the first time on writing, so I am incorporating every detail. So, yeah...I was shocked to see my name up there. Aniket showed me the mail and started hurling abuses at me. The asshole should have realised that once we had been great buddies. He could have come any time and asked me bluntly instead. But then everyone wants to be a bloody Tom Cruise on a Mission Impossible and that too with an endless number of sequels! All of them had the intelligence to send the mail but no one thought of analysing the reply to the mail. My name came up there and everyone thought Rahul was the one to spread the lie. My foot! If I had really been the culprit, I wouldn't have placed anything there that was genuinely mine. Nobody would have. I mean while creating the password for the fake account, for example, I would have rather placed 'anikettheasshole' than 'rahul-therockstar'. Aadi was right in gauging earlier that only a fool would have fallen for such a trap which was lame enough. Obviously, the one actually operating the account wasn't a fool and thus trapped me into this. Son of a bitch!

And then…when I heard some of the other reasons that confirmed my involvement, I just couldn't prevent myself from laughing. The best one was, "Rahul never told us that Mallya was his girlfriend." Holy crow, how was that related to my sending the obnoxious SMS to Aniket? Bullshit, they all are big assholes…okay, their sizes vary but still a hole is a hole! Brains are the last things to be found inside their skulls. When a chick as hot as Mallya becomes your girlfriend, and then she asks you to refrain from breaking the news to anyone, how can you say a 'no'? Anything for you ma'am! I cannot show you up here but I know how it feels when one sees that curvy body plunging closer to you. Even the last time when we kissed and my hand pushed inside her T-shirt…flip! Why am I telling you that? This is what nobody understood. I was getting all I wanted just in return for not telling anything to anyone. Aadvitya used his non-existent brains too far and thus made a point out of this. He should have known how it felt to be kissed...after all, he had not even the experience of a guy (oops)! I am also told that it was his girlfriend who said the three precious words to him ahead of him. Such a loser!

Anyway...no more leg pulling, otherwise he won't let me do this important thing.

So it wasn't me! It wasn't Aadi for sure! Manu couldn't have been the one and Aniket's integrity was not questionable. Obviously, it had to be Parv (you already guessed that? Wow...intelligent!). I knew it was him. Manu believed that it was him. Aadi had some idea that it could be him. It was just Aniket who was blind. For him, it was I who was involved. I had to make sure that the view was changed.

It all started with Aadi giving me a call one day. It had been almost a month since we had talked last and I was surprised when he called me up. He wasn't sure whether he should trust me or not but that was enough for me. I was relieved. This was one opening that I was looking for and it came my way. I grabbed it with both my hands. I had to make it count. Frankly speaking, I never had any idea of where to find the beginning of the thread which I was going to hold to reach the end of it. I knew that if somehow I could catch hold of the inception, the other things would follow automatically. It was just like riding a bike, of which we know the critical parts like putting it in the first gear to make it move and then coordinate the accelerator with the release of the clutch. The other gears are followed easily. Just one chapter and I already sound like an author, don't I?

I did nothing special; just got inspired from a couple of cheap B-grade Hindi films and started following our person in question. There was nothing substantial to mention in the first few days except that I got scolded unceasingly at home for staying out too much. It was my Board year and I had to be serious and all that blah...blah! Who was to explain to them that my character was being questioned and there was nothing bigger than that. So after a few days, things came to be noticed. It seemed we weren't the only persons that he hung out with. There was a certain bunch of college students with whom he used to chill out at a specific time in the day. There were specific places which these people visited with Parv and did specific things that included smoking and drinking. As far as my knowledge went, Parv wasn't known to smoke. A person with a tumour in the brain was supposed to keep away from all this and it was this that got my brain to move first. There was certainly something suspicious about all this and surely my first clue towards entrapping the man!

I told Aadi about this and initially he was a bit apprehensive about it, but later I convinced him to do what I wanted. He asked Parv for his tumour reports on the pretext of referring them to another doctor for getting a second opinion. Parv, as expected, hesitated but upon repeated pressure, gave up and handed over the report. The report was from an unknown hospital in Ajmer and had a couple of X-rays attached that showed various portions of a human skull. The thing that was written inside the report was impossible for a layman to decipher. Aadi was satisfied and asked me not to play with the sentiments of a dying person any more. I wasn't still convinced because the reports did not mention anywhere that the person was about to die. I rang up the hospital's number given on the top right corner of the report but the call never materialised as it was invalid. I tried googling the name of the hospital but nothing came up and thus out of despair, I forwarded the entire report to Ankit's Dad who happened to be a doctor at Ajmer (Ankit was that fat guy who was Parv's roommate) and I had to wait for some time for the expected to arrive. Thus,

Doubt number 1 on Parv – pending

My status as an asshole – intact

The other peculiar thing that I noted about him was that he visited a particular cyber café at least once or twice a week. I never found him using the computers but he used to go, sit there and have a quick chat with the owner of the café. The café provided facilities like recharging of mobiles as also the internet facility. After a bit of intelligent enquiry from the surrounding shops, I learnt the name of the café owner to be Matka Bhai. I know you have forgotten who he was. Well, he was the same person who was called to break open the locks at the school when Aadi was helping his childhood friend in stealing the examination paper. How do I know this? Well…you aren't the only one to read this story!

I carefully chose the days when Parv wasn't there and entered the café only on those particular days. The café had six computers installed and my only aim was to check out each of them since I had already checked out Parv's PC at the hostel and found nothing extraordinary. That wasn't a problem as each computer was installed in a separate cabin. I was not sure initially whether Matka Bhai recognised me but his disinterested look on the first day of entering the café made it clear that he had not recognised me. So I began going there every possible day and made sure that I did not sit on the same computer again. It took me ten days to work my plan out and check each computer minutely so as to ensure if I could find any clue there. But there was nothing that I could place my finger on and say, "This is it!" I was terribly dejected on the last day when leaving the café. There was no evidence that I could gather despite toiling for so many days and the world ahead seemed dim. I was about to jot down my departure time in the records register when I saw Aniket's phone number in the preceding row. Parv's name was written against it and a 500 rupee recharge had been made on that number, just five minutes earlier. Matka Bhai was smoking a beedi *outside the café which was somewhat empty. I sensed the opportunity to flip through the pages of the records register. A couple of minutes of rapid observation led me to notice the five records of Aniket's cell phone being recharged in the name of Parv and one record of Aadi's cell phone being recharged, again on Parv's name. I had got it! I quickly returned to the page where my entry was supposed to be filled, paid the amount to Matka Bhai on leaving and wondered if this was to lead me to any consequential sequence. I had one satisfaction deep inside – that at least I had something to tell Aadi. Just about when I was to call him and inform him about the little cake, I received another cherry to decorate the cake with. A call from Doctor uncle conveyed what I expected! Thus,*

Doubt number 1 on Parv – cleared (he wasn't having the tumour…rascal!)

Doubt number 2 – raised after doubt 1, pending

My status as an asshole – about to be changed!

It did not take me much to convince Aadi about this! I let him talk to the doctor who discarded the report as just a copy-paste from Wikipedia (that general reference guide). For our satisfaction, we browsed through Wikipedia and typed in 'brain tumour'. Every damn thing that was written in the report matched the words on the screen. I loved the look I saw on Aadi's face. Actually, I had the same look maybe – the timid look that said it all; that we had been mocked at. This had definitely got Aadi going. I told him about his and Aniket's names in the records register and he told me about the free recharges that were being offered by Parv. It did not take us even seconds to make out that the recharges weren't free or hacked; they were being paid out by Parv to Matka Bhai. I had finally found another believer in me and that was Aadi. He finally believed me to be clean and apologised for everything. I slapped him in return though it was revenge for the one that he had planted on my face earlier. He wanted to break the news regarding Parv as quickly as possible to Aniket but I stopped him because we still did not have enough evidence against him. Portions of the messages had yet to be traced and he suggested that it had primarily to do with Matka Bhai most probably, since he had a cyber café and was known to Parv. The very act of duplicating the keys at the school brought him under suspicion. I had missed something, but what was it? I had checked every public computer in the café but there was nothing incriminating that I could find. It was pretty much evident that they had not done anything on a public sharing zone and the proof had to be somewhere in private. There had to be a weak link somewhere.

I went to the café again this time, in the afternoon, accompanied by Manu. Two to tango was any time better than one to waltz. I had wished to take Aadi, but fearing that he might get recognised by Matka Bhai, we decided against it. The plan was pretty simple. Manu had to keep Matka Bhai engaged, out of the shop somehow, while we would carry out the search inside the café without being noticed. He was waiting for us outside the café when we reached there. This made Manu's task that much easier as he did not have to drag him out of the café. It was all up to me now. Since we had gone there in the afternoon, I expected the café to be least crowded and fortunately enough, there was no one that day. I wrote down my entry time in the records register and double checked the register once again. There was nothing worth noting this time around. I looked out of the glass window of the café and saw Manu keeping Matka Bhai engaged in some discussion. I slowly moved towards the master computer that lay on the owner's table. The screensaver in large fonts was showing the name of the café swinging from one corner of the screen to the other. I moved the mouse to disrupt the screensaver and the display returned to the idle screen. I knew what to do next as I was familiar with the computers of the café. I opened the internet explorer, typed 'www.rediff.com' in the address bar and waited for the page to load. I moved the mouse pointer on the loaded page towards the empty box that provided the space to enter the user name and password. I tried for the same user name as given in the mail and the same that I had tried putting in all the other computers of the café. As soon as I typed the 'j' letter of the email id, the page gave me the option of auto filling the space with the id 'jai_malothra'. This was it! This showed that once before the account had been operated from this computer and that's why the option to auto fill was coming up. This was the place from where the messages were being sent. I closed down the window and searched around the computer for any other evidence, but there was none. I looked outside but Manu was busy with Matka Bhai. He gave me the thumbs up signal to carry on further with my work. I searched around the café and inside the owner's table and its drawers one by one, but there was nothing apart from a Nokia 1100 cell phone. I was about to go outside when I noticed that the phone wasn't locked with a code and thus I could access for analysing. I gave a brief glance outside and quickly opened the phonebook of the cell phone. I started scrolling through the contact list. Expectedly, Parv's name was given there. I moved into the SMS folder and saw the SMS from Parv's cell phone. I checked out one after the other and saw that every little SMS received by Aniket was in the inbox of this cell phone and every SMS had the sender's name as Parv. Now all we needed to do was to confront Matka Bhai. As soon as I came out, Manu and I caught hold of Matka Bhai and began to question him. He did put up some resistance but the mere mention of the police was enough to bring him to his knees. He spilled out all the beans. The story was pretty clear. Failing to get close to anyone of us, Parv devised this unique way to dismantle everything and cleverly become our friend. The brain tumour was just an act and he wasn't going to die automatically without our help. He used to send the troublesome messages to Matka Bhai who in turn forwarded them to Aniket through his internet. So Parv being there or not with Aniket did not matter; it was his cell phone that was instrumental in doing the dirty work and he was paying Matka Bhai money for that. Bloody black ass! It did not take long for Aniket and Aadi to arrive on the scene and hear the entire story personally from Matka Bhai. Yeah, Aniket had to apologise to me but I was happy that we all were back together as friends.

Thus doubts number 1, 2, 3, etc. were cleared about Parv and proved that he had been an ass!

My status as an asshole – c'mon, you have read everything above! I am clean!

By the way, did I tell you that Parv actually was interested in Aadi? Or could you guess it? I must tell you a new twist in the story. Remember Aadi failing in chemistry and getting a supplementary? Yeah, that one! Did I ever mention that it was Parv who did that to get closer to his love! Sshhhh...don't tell Aadi about this...let him remain poor at chemistry...

* * * * *

I am sure you wouldn't have liked Rahul. Well, okay if you had, it wouldn't have mattered. The most satisfying fact was that we finally had true evidence on the actual culprit. Now I will let Rahul describe the entire event as he was the one closest to everything and can explain better (actually, he was complaining to me that I had given him very little footage, so I am giving him a separate little space here). Aniket's Dad took good care of Matka Bhai and we made sure that the news would reach Parv's ears. After all, there wouldn't have been greater joy than to see him caught napping. Now each of us was raring for Parv's blood. Since the school was off for the winter break, we decided to catch him away from school.

"Come to Nahargarh at 4 in the evening. Aadi and I are reaching together. I need some fresh air to breathe," Aniket told him on the mobile as we got ready. Nahargarh was perfect as it was a secluded place, devoid of crowds. It was exactly 4 o'clock when we saw Parv's bike ascend the hill. As soon as he parked his bike and took off his helmet, Rahul and Manu, who had hidden behind a rock, came out. He for once had a terrified look on his face but he maintained his composure as he said, "Good, I get to see everyone here, *sahib.* It seems like a different day today." His eyes rolled and his dark body made my mind fill with revulsion.

"Why did you do it?" Aniket screamed at him.

"What *sahib*?" Parv replied.

"You should know better!" Aniket said.

"Oh, that? You know that? Now what about it?" he asked, giving an ugly grin and making a mockery of us. There was arrogance writ large over his face.

"Fucker! You dare to ask that? Bloody black, gay mother fucker, tell me quick the reason for doing so before I tear you into pieces," Aniket replied, moving menacingly towards him.

"Gay? I knew it," I smirked.

"What *sahib?* I have been making an ass out of you since long and still you didn't get it! Simple, I wanted to fuck your life…it's as simple as that. Now hail my genius and live and let live a happy-ever-after life."

"You gay bitch… " Aniket yelled and rushed towards him as we followed behind. Parv did not get a chance to move. I cannot remember at what all points on his body we hit him, but he lay flat on the ground as we kept on kicking him. I used all of my body's force to make mince meat out of him. His nonchalant attitude made us angrier still and we gave full vent to the frustration simmering inside us. We wanted to leave visible marks on his body which would remind him for some time what we had done to him. When we found no resistance being offered by him, we left him there on the ground, walked to our bikes and left. We could hear him scream Aniket's name for once.

"Fuck off, you gay bastard." came Aniket's reply to his scream! I loved the use of the 'gay' word by him.

"*Oye* Aadi…I believe you two kissed each other?"

I had started my bike when Manu's words hit my ears. His words struck at my festering wound and I switched off the engine of my bike. I parked my bike on the side stand and went again to Parv when he was trying to stand up on his legs. He looked up at me and I, with all the remaining force that I could gather, slammed a punch on his face right close to his lips. A loud thud was produced as he collapsed, writhing in pain. I wiped off his blood stain on my fist, turned back and shook my head in disgust with everyone staring at me.

"Let's go," I said.

20

Endings are Beautiful

I woke up the next morning, thinking that it would probably be the last morning to wake up like that and hoping that no such morning would follow ever. I hoped it would mark the end that day of all our farewells, when we would no longer be called school students. It was going to be the official kick! Up till now I had been feeling the vibrations of anxiety in my belly, probably similar to those what a newlywed bride must feel. You desperately wait for the day which should turn out to be the most beautiful day of your life but the feeling of uneasiness is invariably present, as you feel unsure about your future. Actually it's a mixed feeling of apprehension as well as anticipation. You are frightened to leave behind all your pleasant past and look forward to a bright future ahead.

As for me, I had no such mixed feelings within me, instead all I could feel was pain – pain at leaving the place and not seeing it again probably; pain of not wearing the same uniform ever again; pain of not being forced to listen to the bugging alarm bell ring every morning; pain of not seeing such wonderful friends again; pain of not seeing her again sit close to the window seat. Everything! It was like I was going to lose everything that had by now become an integral part of my life. There was no spring in my walk as I climbed down from my bed. It was raining outside and I could not decide whether to rejoice or feel sad. It wasn't beautiful in any case. Rainfall at the fag end of January can definitely be a pain in the ass, firstly, because it means wearing extra layers of clothes on your body to ward off the cold due to the steep fall in temperature and second, it was adding to the frustration already plaguing my heart.

I resignedly put on my woollen blazer specially made for the day. I had passed the previous week in mixing and matching my clothes. My Mom wanted me to look the best on that day – the day when her son was leaving a world that he simply adored. How could I look the best with a dejected heart inside? Still I chose a black blazer to wear with the black corduroy trousers of mine – black, the colour of mourning!

Aniket blew the horn of his Dad's car on reaching my house, to pick me up. I came down and saw Rahul and Manu seated inside the car. It was a sensible idea to bring the car as the rain was liable to spoil all our plans. It was good to find that the rain had turned into a drizzle by now and everyone looked his or her best; at least they tried to look so. Aniket had rubbed in a lot of gel into his hair to make them defy the pull of gravity, while Rahul had a series of lockets hanging around his neck and was looking like Pierce Bronson with his chest hair visible through his deliberately unbuttoned shirt. Manu looked the same as on other days, except for the fact that he had worn a blazer over his shirt. There was exchange of glad greetings as I entered the car. As expected, everyone was in high spirits. I felt good as this was supposed to take my mind off all the depressing thoughts troubling my mind. Being with them meant the world to me at that moment.

The auditorium was already full to the brim when we entered. It was humming with people's voices. Arrangements were being made by Class XI students, while the faculty was trying to guide them from behind. Mr. Chaturvedi was looking as lost as ever while Miss Chandrakanta was trying to put her finger in every pie. Mr. Maths, Mr. Physical Education and Mr. Physics were seated in the front row, looking completely unconcerned with the goings on. I looked around the auditorium and noticed Class XII girls decked up to the hilt in colourful sarees. I rubbed my eyes with disbelief and looked again, trying to decipher who was who. Girls whom I daily saw in school uniforms were looking so different now. Some were wearing backless or single-stringed or halter-neck blouses to match all kinds of sarees. My girl was yet to arrive but the girls from my section looked so much better now. Obviously the girls from the commerce section looked hotter than ever before. I glanced at myself and at the other three standing with me and felt that the guys could never look different! Rahul stood with Mallya and oh man! she looked smoking hot with her entire back on display. It seemed so feathery smooth and fair. Now I could fathom why Rahul was not willing to reveal his feelings for Mallya and attract other male eyes towards her. While searching for chairs to sit, I glanced up on the stage and found one junior girl bending down to catch hold of a wire lying on the floor. Absolutely unaware of her posture, she was giving us a full display of those perfectly shining and uncovered legs, thanks to her short skirt. I moved my eyes to land them on the hotties from the commerce section as they seemed nothing in comparison to those legs in the short skirt. Gosh! I was going to miss this all.

Okay, I forget to tell you that not only I, even the other boys were glancing at every other girl's legs. How else were we expected to pass our time while waiting for the function to begin? Anyway, it is not easy to ignore a temptation!

We all sat next to each other, waiting for the event to begin. I looked around but there was no sign of her yet. I was desperate to see her. With every other girl looking pretty that day, I felt she must be looking like a show-stopper. We had been talking about this day for over a month and so I had no idea what she was going to wear. There was no sign of her yet, but I had no other option than to wait for her to arrive. Meanwhile I noticed people coming and greeting each other. I also noticed that Parv hadn't arrived but then his absence was better any day than his presence. A hesitant Vyom was seen hugging Dushyant; an irritating Shakti was niggling Shivam; a rowdy Naveen was pushing Suresh and everybody was behaving like a busybody. These were people about whom I would not have cared but they were names which were going to be etched in my memory forever. I also knew that most of them would not find my name on my interaction list in the life ahead but their mere presence made them seem important.

"Ahh…there she is," said Manu, close to my ears.

"Where?" I asked, looking frantically around to catch a glimpse of her. Manu pointed his finger in her direction, inadvertently blocking my view of her. I pushed it down irritatingly, so that my eyes could feast on her looks. At last my eyes fell on my Venus. Yeah…she was the one. My heart started to play the song, '*You're beautiful…*' as sung by James Blunt. She looked like a goddess standing at the auditorium door and clad in a pink and blue *bandhej* saree *(she later told me that it was* bandhej). Her blouse wasn't entirely backless but revealed quite a large portion of her back. Her cheeks looked prettier, her nose looked cuter and her eyes spoke volumes. I stood absolutely smitten by her beauty! It was the classroom door where I had first seen her and it seemed as though it was only yesterday that I had seen her for the first time. She looked simply stunning and gorgeous as ever. She saw me stare at her and we exchanged a silent 'hello' through our eyes. We had got pretty used to such silent greetings. Through subtle gestures I conveyed to her that she looked awesome. She mouthed her thanks and moved to find a chair amongst the girls' row. I rested my back against the chair and let out a sigh. She was one great thing to have happened in the past one year.

Sum1 is lukin cute and handsum! – N

I saw her message on my cell phone and turned to look at her. As expected, she was looking at me, possibly trying to find out my reaction. I sent thanks in reply and smiled towards her. She smiled back. My heart did a somersault and I promptly turned my face away. I knew that if I looked at her a moment longer, tears could start flowing from my eyes at the thought of getting separated from her. Emotions were at their peak and it was getting difficult for me to control myself. Seeing me unduly silent, Rahul and Aniket asked me again and again if I was not feeling well but I told them that I was fine. There was nothing wrong with me, was it?

Madam Grace Pinto (our Director's better half) lighted the candles kept in front of Jesus' large mural in the auditorium as our principal assisted her and that marked the inauguration of the ceremony. It also was a signal for Class XI students to display their creative and artistic abilities through their (*boring and uninspired*) performances. The next hour passed with everyone either yawning or looking sideways to exchange some rumour or gossip. There was activity on the stage but who cared! This was always considered the sad part of the equally sad farewell – useless and crappy performances by juniors to show that they cared for us while in reality, it was an occasion for them to celebrate, for they would no longer have any seniors above them. Our collars were pinned up with roses as Madam Grace invited us to the stage to exchange pleasantries with us. Silence prevailed in the auditorium for the first time. There was this strange aura around as if time stood still and the world had come to a halt. It was not just because she held a position of authority but because there was something about her personality which commanded respect. She began to chant the name of Jesus Christ with her eyes closed and I could feel the presence of something divine there. Everything was quiet and still around me. I tried pushing Manu sideways jokingly, but he nudged me to stop me from fooling around. Another two minutes of group meditation and then she began her speech, "Dear children, or maybe I should not use the word here because my children are moving to the next level today…they aren't children any more. As Jesus has brought you all up till here, I would like to tell you about…" and she went on and on.

*The ten minutes of sitting idle and listening to talks made my mind enter the nostalgia mode. The blur in front of my eyes again took me away from the present and my cerebrum returned to an ocean of the past. This was not the case with me alone; everyone around too had entered into another time zone. I began to relive the past that I had lived in the school and scenes of Rahul standing with me at the classroom door, Aniket sitting with me in the classroom to listen to the chemistry lecture with Parv (*ewww*), Miss Chandrakanta teaching in the adjoining class and we all peeping through the window or fighting for the basketball to cast an impression on the junior girls, I holding Noopur's hand inside the girls' washroom (*who shot this?*), we, the Page 3 celebrities of the college magazine, having girls fall over and chant our names over and over again and Rahul…Rahul…*

"Rahul…the best boy of the school!" came the announcement.

Wait…how did this come about? When did this happen?

I heard applause and Aniket whistle as I was shaken out of my reverie. The compere announced Rahul's name as the year's best boy of the school. He had already reached the stage, flashing the million-dollar smile while holding the prize proudly as he received from Madam Grace.

"What the…? Partiality…," Manu said, and we both tried to ignore the moment by refusing to clap in appreciation. I wouldn't have minded getting the prize. There were a few more prizes that were awarded but we received none. I wished I had done something to be able to avail the opportunity of standing on the stage in front of everybody. However, there was one redeeming feature of it all and that was we all could get ourselves photographed with Rahul and the trophy. I could always fool my children and grandchildren by saying that their Dad or Grandad as the case would be, received the best boy award. Cleverness does pay!

There were only two sounds emerging from the dining area where lunch was being served before we all parted ways. One could hear the clatter of forks and knives as also the frequent clicking of the camera. I had filled up my plate with the maximum amount of food that was on offer and was ensuring that I remained in the focus of the camera. There was no scope left for display of emotions, so it was better to catch up with others and concentrate on the delicious food. I had exchanged my vote of thanks with everyone; after all, one gets only one chance to say farewell in school life…you see.

"So Mr. Handsome…no time to catch up with me…*hun*?" I was posing with some of the guys when I heard Noopur's voice from behind.

"I thought we weren't supposed to talk in school," I said, moving away from everyone and replying in a low tone. Everybody was busy with their own business and I guessed nobody noticed us talking.

"Yeah…this is the last day and no one can do anything now," she said smilingly.

"Ohh…yeah, right. Last day…the last day…shit…it's the last day," I wailed.

"You could have come up to me. It's the last day. Will you always remain such a jerk?" she asked in a complaining voice. Her lips curled together as she went on complaining while my eyes were focused on her pink lipstick, which looked damn sexy on her lips. That pink and blue sari seemed to be made exclusively for her body and I could bet there was nothing better or hotter around than her exposed slim waist.

"Do you know that you look fantabulous today?" I said. Frankly speaking, she was looking absolutely astounding *(don't ask me when she didn't?).*

"How can you even steal my dialogues? You can never be original, can you? You could have let me say that first…jerk," she complained again. I could have cuddled her to death there and then. I wished I could go down on my knees and keep staring at her face. Every little face that she made was too cute for me to handle. People had started noticing us stand together and talk. I even noticed Manu making faces from a distance. Mr. Physical Education was keeping a constant watch on us as I noticed from the corner of my eyes.

"We are hogging the limelight, I guess…" I said, drawing close to her.

"So…shall we disappear?" she said and winked.

We moved out and made our way down the stairs to reach the basement. It wasn't so tough a task to get away from the crowd and be in peace and seclusion. She stood on one side of the classroom, taking support of the wall while I stood supporting myself against the opposite one.

"I haven't been to this place ever," she said, panting due to the climb down the innumerable steps.

"I never took you to private places on dates, you see."

"Aha…what are your plans Mr. Handsome?" she asked, looking around to check if anyone was coming.

"I never made a plan to come here," I said, moving to the opposite side.

"I cannot expect good things from you…ah...what?" she looked up towards me when I was just a few inches away from her.

"Sshhh..." I whispered. There was complete silence for long after that. My right hand whirled around her waist, slowly holding her tight. She was feeling cold, I could feel that. She wasn't moving and I was controlling myself. The distance between us decreased slowly with every passing moment. I could inhale the fragrance emerging from her hair as I stroked them with my left hand. My right hand clasped her round the waist, my lips moved closer to hers and I could feel my heart beat violently. Her breathing increased and I could feel her warm breath against my face. She kept her eyes closed, anticipating the moment. She looked a little baby with those closed eyes, conscious of something alien happening. I moved further down and our lips locked in a kiss. My eyes closed of their own accord. The world had disappeared, the ground beneath my feet had moved and time had come to a halt. A precious moment had been created! (Well…my kids would certainly be proud of their Dad now…I had received a kiss on the farewell day!)

"This lipstick actually tastes so damn good," I said biting her lips before breaking away from her clasp.

"Shut up…it's not about the lipstick," she screamed, punching me on my stomach before we locked our lips again. The next time when we separated, we both were panting due to lack of air inside our lungs. Who said endings cannot be perfect? I realised I wasn't leaving a world out here; I was carrying it along with me to the future. I had already spent a good part of my life here and the memories were going to remain with me for the rest of my life…unplugged! No one was parting for ever. We were just carrying life forward with us into different zones but at the same time. She was still close to me and they all were upstairs. We were just moving up the ladder of life…wasn't she beautiful? Wasn't the time spent with all of them beautiful? Wasn't this all beautiful?

"Shall we go now?" I asked and wiped off the lipstick mark that had been stamped on my lips.

"How dare you remove that?"

And my lips were sealed with her lips on hers again…

Dear, I Love You

by Arun Sabtharishi

Price	:	Rs. 125
Pages	:	208
Size	:	5.25 × 7.75 inches
Binding	:	Paperback
Language	:	English
Subject	:	Fiction/Romance
ISBN	:	9788183520874

About the book:

A guy sees a girl, falls in love… woos and wins her love. They both experience the ecstasy of love that develops between them and both realise the purport of love. They discover that love is blind, literally blind against anything in the world. The guy makes a mistake; he seeks forgiveness from the girl. The girl too commits a mistake. Again the guy seeks apologies from her. Does the girl forgive the guy modestly for the mistake SHE has made?

Beyond just hormone secretion or the chemical reaction that takes place in the human body, love is something more. Trust... hope...life...

This is a story of love, affection, bliss, blues, hassles and harmony between a guy and his girl when both are forced to acknowledge, "Dear, I love you!"

Let's Get Committed...

by Smita & Utkarsh

Price	:	Rs. 125
Pages	:	240
Size	:	5.0 × 7.75 inches
Binding	:	Paperback
Language	:	English
Subject	:	Fiction/Romance
ISBN	:	9788183520157

About the book:

Hierarchy of modern age love:

Orkut > Chatting > Phone > CCD > Movies

Apurv and Radhika get committed. They try to adjust to their new marital status committed by proving the equation 1+1=1.

~ Facebook status = In a relationship…Orkut status: committed.

~ In a given area, low population density implies hands together & lesser, lips and cheeks.

~ 1st testimonial from him/her…scrapbook full of sweetheart/love.

~ Desktop wallpaper = "C:\my pictures\my.sweetheart.jpg"

This stage relates to the fact that even after liking each other, they just experiment with the concept of being together and not because of love… just in hope that they might (if it's written) fall in it.

Being a hottie, Radhika initially misses the single tag and the direct and indirect benefits associated with it. Apurv tries to reinstate the feeling of love in her but fails…though partially…

Life goes on as time tests their compatibility and then suddenly destiny shows its darker side…

Radhika is gone…

What happens next….

If it's love, will it cease to exist if they are apart?

Does Apurv find a new love?

Take One More Chance
by Shriya Garg

Price : Rs. 125
Pages : 256
Size : 5.0 × 7.75 inches
Binding : Paperback
Language : English
Subject : Fiction/Comedy
ISBN : 9788183520140

About the book:

Naina Kashyap's to-do List:

1. Change career.
2. Next time the guy at McDonald's acts stupid—be polite. Don't get him arrested again. Stupidity is not a crime. Unfortunately.
3. Change society's notion towards child labour.
4. Dad wants me to get married. What the___?
   Also remember to change family.

Some people always take the right decisions and some people take decisions and then make them right.

Naina Kashyap was so sure that she fell in the second category. A sharp-tongued, career-oriented girl of today, she had an opinion about everything—from the local underprivileged children forced to work as labourers to her parents' if-I-am-Jesus-Christ-then-you-are-Paris-Hilton marriage.

So when her father ordered her to find a decent groom for herself, she responded in the only way she knew how—rebellion. From crazy accidents in Delhi's streets to near drowning in kiddie pools, she rained her wrath on every man she came across.

She thought that things could never get worse. Little did she know that the drama had only just begun.

Just Friends...

by Sumrit Shahi

Price	:	Rs. 125
Pages	:	264
Size	:	5.0 × 7.75 inches
Binding	:	Paperback
Language	:	English
Subject	:	Fiction/Romance
ISBN	:	9788183520119

National Bestseller

About the book:

He knows everything about her, right from her favourite books to her favourite bra.

She knows everything about him, right from his favourite soccer club to his favourite x rated websites.

He will complete her English homework, even at three in the night.

She will arrange an Armani suit for him, even if it calls for flirting with ugly guys.

He has her picture in his wallet.

She has his number on speed dial.

They talk to each other all the time.

They talk about each other when they don't talk to each other.

They discuss everything from periods to playstation.

They have tasted alcohol and then thrown up...together.

They have bunked countless tuitions... together.

They can't live without each other.

YET

They don't love each other.

They are JUST FRIENDS...

'Just Friends' is funny, honest, sad and straight from the heart.

—The Indian Express